WORK AND LOVE

"These will be fine stables," Juan said.

Charlotte's eyes glistened with excitement. "Yes, they will, won't they?"

Juan gave her a gentle smile. "Why don't you do that more often?" he asked.

"Do what?"

"Be yourself. You are quite likable, you know, when you are not playing games."

Charlotte stiffened. "You call them games, others call them manners. Something you, obviously, don't know anything about."

She turned from him and began marching back the way she had come. She had not gone more than ten paces when she felt Juan's hand on her shoulder.

He spun her around, their eyes met and held. Charlotte felt herself move forward and felt Juan's lips on hers. . . .

TEXAS
PROMISES
BOOK III

Hidden Longings

Marie Lindquist

BANTAM BOOKS
TORONTO · NEW YORK · LONDON · SYDNEY · AUCKLAND

RL 6, IL age 12 and up

HIDDEN LONGINGS
A Bantam Book / August 1987

*The Starfire logo of a stylized star are registered
trademarks of Bantam Books, Inc. Registered in U.S. Patent and
Trademark Office and elsewhere.*

ISBN 0-553-26668-3

Published simultaneously in the United States and Canada

*Bantam Books are published by Bantam Books, Inc. Its trade-
mark, consisting of the words "Bantam Books" and the por-
trayal of a rooster, is Registered in U.S. Patent and Trademark
Office and in other countries. Marca Registrada. Bantam
Books, Inc., 666 Fifth Avenue, New York, New York 10103.*

PRINTED IN THE UNITED STATES OF AMERICA

O   0 9 8 7 6 5 4 3 2 1

Hidden Longings

Chapter One

Charlotte Harmon frowned at her reflection in the mirror, unable to decide which of the two lengths of fabric would make her the most beautiful.

"Will you want the lilac, then?" the dressmaker, Madame Leblanc, inquired.

Charlotte let the blue sprigged fabric fall to her feet in an elegant heap. Stretching out her hand, she took the lilac cloth Madame had been holding. With a few expert gestures she fluffed and folded the material into the lines of a tight-waisted dress. There were just these two lengths left, the lilac and the blue sprigged, of the last shipment from New Orleans. Madame Leblanc had instructions to make them into gowns, one for Charlotte and one for her half sister, Teyah.

"What do you think, Teyah?" Charlotte asked, although she sensed her half sister's thoughts were far from dresses and fabric.

Teyah had been gazing out the window, her attention focused on the vast reaches of Cielo Hermoso. "Take whichever one you want, Charlotte," Teyah responded, her pale blond hair catching the sun as she turned away from the window. "I don't care."

I don't care. That was Teyah for you, so deeply in love with Cleve that she didn't even care what she wore.

Charlotte stared at Teyah as if she were a being from another planet. *Imagine,* she thought, letting go of the sprigged material and picking up the lilac again, *imagine, being so dazzled by someone that you don't even care what you wear!*

Even so, there was that little nagging doubt in her mind. *Love.* Why was everyone falling in love except her? Charlotte was used to being just a little bit happier than everyone else, used to being just a little bit richer and just a little bit more sought after. She didn't mind if other people had nice things, just as long as she had *more* of them. Now she felt the scales tipping, and she didn't like it one bit.

What is love, anyway? she puzzled, pulling a thick, honey-gold curl forward to see how it would look against the lilac fabric. Teyah said it was having feelings for someone that were so strong they almost swept you away. But the only person Charlotte had ever had strong feelings for was Juan Ortiz, and those feelings, she was quite certain, had nothing at all to do with love.

Juan Ortiz. Even the echo of his name in her mind triggered an avalanche of feelings. He was handsome, possibly the most handsome young man she'd ever seen, with bold dark eyes and high cheekbones and a slim, hard-muscled body. But he was arrogant too. She'd danced with him once at a party and still remembered the way he'd looked at her, still remembered the firm, exciting way he'd held her in his arms, as if she belonged to him alone.

And who was Juan Ortiz, anyway? The nearby ranch he and his father owned was no the dance.

Suddenly Charlotte
her eyes in the mirror, sea-green eyes
her thick golden hair and creamy white skin,
were her best feature.

"I must be going crazy," she said aloud, turning to Madame Leblanc with a decisive smile. "Lilac will never, *never* go with my eyes. Make my gown the blue sprigged one. And please be careful about the waist. Last time it was much too tight."

"Mademoiselle wants to be fashionable," Madame Leblanc reminded Charlotte, her long face devoid of expression.

"Yes," Charlotte said, wading out of the tide of fabric, "but I want to breathe too."

There were guests at dinner that night, but that was not unusual. George and Lavinia Harmon liked guests, and a big ranch like Cielo Hermoso could accommodate lots of them. Tonight two extra places were set, for a rancher from Dallas named Nate Briscoe and his son, Billy Joe. Like most young men who visited Cielo Hermoso, twenty-year-old Billy Joe was eager to sit across the table from Charlotte and flirt with her. The unusual thing was that Charlotte, contrary to her reputation, was not at all interested in flirting back.

"Do you feel all right?" Teyah questioned, studying her half sister.

"Of course I feel all right," Charlotte replied.

, said Billy Joe Briscoe, "is some fresh air. Night ride under the stars'd fix you up just fine."

It was clear what Billy Joe had in mind, even to Charlotte, who hadn't been paying all that much attention to him. "I don't *need* fixing up," she said, a trace of irritation in her voice. "Why is everyone making such a fuss?"

"There, now," said Billy Joe with an undefeated smile, "see how edgy you are? I'll ask your pa if we can go riding."

"No, no, no!" Charlotte said sharply.

She knew she was being rude to Billy Joe. He was a guest, after all, and his father was thinking about buying breeding stock from Cielo Hermoso. But there was a limit to how much one person could stand. In her short time on earth, less than eighteen years, Charlotte had gone riding with entirely too many Billy Joes. And what had it gotten her? Nothing but a bored, restless feeling, a feeling that made her want to do something that would shock everyone at the table.

"Cleve and I will go riding with you tomorrow," Teyah told the disappointed Billy Joe. "Cleve knows all the wonderful places on Cielo Hermoso. We'd love to show them to you."

Teyah's eyes sparkled. *We'd love to show them to you.* Charlotte was sure that Teyah's heart wasn't as hollow as her own was. Cleve filled it up. Cleve made Teyah's cheeks glow when she said words like *we.*

Suddenly Charlotte crumpled her napkin and flung it down beside her plate. "I guess maybe I'm not feeling well after all," she said and, turning toward the head of the table, asked, "May I be excused, please?"

"If you wish," Lavinia Harmon said. "But we're having lemon bombe, your favorite dessert."

"I don't care," Charlotte replied. She left the room, intending to go upstairs. Instead she slipped out onto the porch, knowing she wouldn't be bothered out there.

The sun was just sinking below the horizon, dragging wisps of pink and yellow and orange clouds down with it. The land, the flat, endless land of Texas, stretched out like a wide sea, shadows gathering between clumps of brush and trees.

For a moment Charlotte felt as if she were alone in the universe. Billy Joe Briscoe had vanished behind her, no more important than an insect. Nothing and no one existed except herself and the beautiful ranch that stretched out on all sides of her. *Cielo Hermoso.* Could any words describe the special feelings the words stirred in her heart? Since she had grown up without a mother, the ranch itself had become a parent to her. She belonged to Cielo Hermoso, just as Cielo Hermoso belonged to her. She would live her whole life here, never needing to stray from its borders. And someday, when she married, the man she loved would live here with her.

Charlotte closed her eyes, trying to see into the future. She saw herself racing across the plains on horseback, a handsome young man at her side. Suddenly a wave of annoyance swept over her. How would she ever find that handsome young man if all the boys she met were like

Billy Joe? *They're all the same,* she thought with a sigh. *They're all so predictable. I know what they're going to say five minutes before they say it.*

Well, she reminded herself, that wasn't quite true. There was one young man who didn't fit the pattern, one young man whose actions she couldn't predict at all. That young man was Juan Ortiz.

There she was thinking of Juan again, something she'd promised herself to stop doing. *As if I cared about him!* she thought vehemently. It's just because there's no one else to think about, she told herself, just because—

"I knew you'd be out here."

The voice startled Charlotte and she turned quickly, just in time to avoid Billy Joe Briscoe's hand on her shoulder. He was good-looking, she thought, but stupid. He reminded her of the broad-backed, small-headed cattle her father bred.

"How did you know that?" she asked, not because she was curious but because she wanted to distract him. She didn't want Billy Joe moving any closer to her in the fragrance-filled twilight.

"Why, I read your signals, of course," Billy Joe answered. "I knew you weren't sick, just pretending, so we could have an excuse to be alone. As soon as we finished eating that lemon boom—"

"Lemon bombe," Charlotte corrected, but Billy Joe didn't miss a beat.

"—I scooted on out here to be with you."

"How wonderful," Charlotte said without enthusiasm.

Her voice was hollow, but that was one signal Billy Joe missed. He took a step closer to her.

"Moon'll be rising soon," he said. "Perfect night for a ride."

"I suppose so," Charlotte replied, moving deftly away from him. She wasn't worried about Billy Joe. She could handle him with both hands tied behind her back.

"Well, then, what do you say?"

"To what?" Charlotte's green eyes glowed at him through the dusk.

Billy Joe was enchanted. "Shall I go to the stable and saddle a horse?"

"One horse?"

"Yes."

Charlotte almost smiled. "If you want to."

Billy Joe whooped with delight. One horse for both of them—she wanted his arms around her as much as he did! he thought. "I'll be right back," he said and, with a meaningful smile, headed off across the yard.

Charlotte watched him go without the slightest twinge of guilt. She hadn't actually said she'd go riding with him. She'd only agreed that yes, it was a perfect night and yes, he could saddle a horse if he wanted to. If he was silly enough to read more into her words than that . . . well, that was *his* problem.

When Billy Joe returned with the saddled horse and found the porch empty, he sat down to wait. Maybe she went to switch her clothes, he told himself, or to fuss with her hair; girls are always doing things like that, especially when they know they're going to get kissed.

He waited a long time, looking up at the stars as they popped out, one by one. He even sang snatches of the cowboy tunes he knew, wondering if he should sing any of them to Charlotte later.

After a long, long time of waiting he began to grow impatient. And angry. Where was she, anyway? Why had she lied to him about going for a ride? Well, he'd have a thing or two to say to her in the morning. Just see if she felt like lying to him *then*.

As Charlotte mounted the stairs to her room, she found herself wondering what would have happened if it had been Juan Ortiz and not Billy Joe Briscoe who'd wanted to go riding with her in the moonlight. *Of course I wouldn't go*, she assured herself. *I wouldn't even consider it*. But Juan wouldn't be fooled as easily as Billy Joe had been. If he wanted to go riding with her, she was sure he'd find a way to do it! The thought, for some strange reason, sent a shiver racing along her spine.

Charlotte came awake abruptly in the middle of the night. She'd been dreaming. Dreaming of . . . she turned in bed, trying to grasp the trailing thread of her dream. Suddenly she saw a flickering square of light dancing on the rose-patterned wallpaper of her room, a square of light that had never been there before.

Charlotte's muscles tensed. The last threads of the dream vanished, gone forever. Something was wrong, terribly wrong. Footsteps were pounding back and forth across the yard, and shouts filled the air.

Throwing back the lace-edged sheets, Charlotte ran to the window and saw, in one horrified glance, why her wall had been aglow with light. The stable was on fire! Flames shot high in the air. Wrenching open the window, she felt heat against her face. Even this far away she could feel the intensity of the flames.

"Get everyone up!" cried a voice in the hallway, her father's. "There's a wind tonight and I'm afraid the roof of the house might catch!"

Fear swirled through Charlotte, fear so hot it seemed to melt every nerve and muscle in her body. It couldn't be—Cielo Hermoso couldn't be in danger! For a moment she stood, gripping the windowsill for support. Then she heard her father's voice again, saying, "Get the hands up, we'll need all the help we can get!"

Automatically Charlotte reached for her clothes. She dressed hastily, so hastily that she forgot to put on all but one of her petticoats. She didn't take time with her hair, either, but tied it back with the first ribbon that came to hand. Yanking open the door, she stepped out into the hallway just as Lavinia was about to knock on her door. "Where's Papa?" Charlotte asked.

Lavinia, still in her dressing gown, looked at her stepdaughter with startled eyes. "The stable is burning," she said, "he and Cleve went—"

Charlotte didn't wait to hear the rest. Lifting her skirts in a most unladylike fashion, she raced down the immense curving staircase that led to the ground floor.

"Charlotte!" Lavinia called behind her. "Whatever are you doing?"

"I'm going to help!" Charlotte called back. Her heart thumped as she ran across the yard, thumped partly in fear and partly because, unused to running, she was out of breath before she'd covered half the distance to the stable. She wouldn't stop, though. Not when the whole future of Cielo Hermoso was at stake.

Chapter Two

Charlotte stood, hypnotized by the flames that roared and leaped before her. One whole end of the stable was burning, and hands were hurrying to bring the frightened, screaming horses out into the yard. Somebody bumped into her, and turning, she saw the face of Billy Joe Briscoe.

"Charlotte!" He was as surprised as she was. "What are you doing out here?" Forgetting how angry he'd been with her a few hours ago, he put his arm protectively around her and started to draw her away.

"What do you think I'm doing here?" she replied brusquely, pulling away from him. "I'm going to help."

It took a while for the message to work its way to Billy Joe's brain. At first, he wasn't sure he'd heard right. "But . . . but you can't. It's dangerous and, well, you *are* a girl, after all."

Charlotte clicked her tongue impatiently against her teeth. She didn't have time to argue with Billy Joe. In one swift movement she ran forward, leaving him behind.

Fortunately, no one else questioned her right to be at the fire. Cleve, busy organizing the hands in a bucket brigade, merely gave her an encourag-

11

ing nod. Her father, worried and distracted, paused just long enough to ask if everyone at the house was safe. Left alone, Charlotte hurried forward, right to the door of the burning stable.

Horses were still being brought out, their nervous cries filling the night air.

"Here!" someone said abruptly, thrusting the end of a lead rope into her hand.

Instinctively, Charlotte grasped the rope. Beyond the silhouette of the horse's muzzle, outlined against the brilliant light, she saw the tense face of Mose Chandler, her father's foreman. "Are we going to lose any of them, Mose?" she questioned.

A muscle in Mose's jaw tensed. "I don't know, Miss Charlotte. We're doing our best."

The idea that even one of their horses might be lost in the flames was more than Charlotte could stand. The horses were one of the things that made Cielo Hermoso the famous ranch it was, and without them . . . well, there wouldn't be a Cielo Hermoso without them. Mose's words propelled her into action. She hurried off with the horse he'd given to her, turning it into a paddock that lay safely out of the fire's path. As soon as the horse was safe, she ran back to the stable.

Charlotte lost track of how many times she ran back and forth that night or how many horses she turned into the paddock. She knew that the hem of her skirt became ripped and torn and that, more than once, someone doused her with water to keep sparks from burning her.

While she and Mose and his men worked to rescue the horses, others worked to control the fire itself. There was a brisk wind from the south, a wind that picked up burning embers and carried them toward the the house. Looking up, Charlotte saw men stationed on the roof of the house, ready to beat out the burning brands before they could catch fire.

The stable was a long, magnificent building that could house almost fifty horses. One look told Charlotte that the building, engulfed in flames, was already lost. There wasn't enough time; and the fire, which had started when a horse kicked a lantern into a bed of straw, was burning out of control. The most Cleve's bucket brigade could do was hold the flames back long enough to rescue the animals inside.

"That's it," Mose finally told Charlotte. He'd always thought of Charlotte, his employer's daughter, as spoiled and pampered and too pretty for her own good. But now, looking at her exhausted, soot-streaked face, he didn't think she was spoiled at all.

"Did we save them all?" Charlotte asked.

"Well . . ."

Her green eyes were as unmelting as sea ice. "Mose, tell me. Did we?"

"There's that colt, Lisette. Too big to carry out and so skittish we can't get her to come." He saw the stricken look on Charlotte's face. "Can't save 'em all, Miss. You did good, just doing what you did."

Before he could stop her, Charlotte darted into the burning stable. Lisette was hers, her property, a foal born to her own mare, Minx. Charlotte couldn't simply abandon her.

Only after she'd entered the stable did Charlotte realize why Mose had given up on Lisette. The overhead beams, in flames, threatened to collapse at any moment. This is going to be an awfully silly way to die, Charlotte thought, trying to save a horse! But she was halfway to Lisette's stall, and so she continued. A burning splinter crashed down beside her, narrowly missed her and setting a pile of baled hay on fire.

"Come on, Lisette," she said, grabbing the filly's halter.

But the animal, terrified, wouldn't budge. Now Charlotte wished she'd spent more time with the filly, wished she'd gotten to know her the way Teyah spent time getting to know her horse, Kwahadi. But horses, to Charlotte, were creatures that someone else cared for and trained. She hadn't planned on having much to do with Lisette until the filly was old enough to ride.

Frantic to make the filly follow her, too stubborn to leave something that belonged to her behind, Charlotte searched her mind for a strategy. An answer occurred to her as she looked into Lisette's eyes. The filly's eyes were enormous with fright. "If you don't like what you see," Charlotte said, "then I'll fix it so you won't have to look."

Swiftly she hiked her skirt up and began unfastening the buttons of her petticoat. It was then that she discovered she was wearing only one underskirt. The idea of appearing before the men in the yard without a petticoat, with her ruined skirt clinging to the outline of her body, shocked her. It didn't shock her enough to stop her, though. Folding the petticoat, she wrapped the cloth around Lisette's head, covering her eyes.

"Maybe now you'll come with me," she said, but Lisette refused to move. Charlotte's heart sank. "Please, Lisette," she urged. "You can't die here. Why, Papa said you're worth at least seven hundred dollars, don't you even care about *that*?"

Lifting one delicate hoof, Lisette stepped forward. She followed Charlotte out of the stable as if it was what she'd been meaning to do all along. Less than two minutes later the roof of the stable collapsed behind them in a shower of sparks.

When George Harmon heard that his daughter had gone into the burning stable, he was furious. And frightened. Charlotte was his only child, the child he'd pampered and spoiled and indulged ever since her mother's capture by the Indians so many years ago.

When her father found her, Charlotte was clinging to Lisette's neck. At first he thought she was clinging out of terror, but coming closer, he saw that she was smiling. She was more than smiling—she was laughing.

"Are you all right, Charlotte?" he asked, his brow furrowing.

"Of course I'm all right, Papa."

"I don't understand why you're laughing."

Charlotte looked at her father, then at Lisette. She couldn't explain to him what had happened in the stable, couldn't explain how Lisette had refused to move until she'd told her she was worth seven hundred dollars. Charlotte was laughing because she and Lisette had a lot in common. Both of them were beautiful, both of them were stubborn, and both of them had a healthy appreciation of their own worth.

The stables were still smoldering when help arrived. Maggie McNeill and Buck Crawford were the first to come, saying that the glow on the horizon had been bright enough to wake them from slumber. Knowing that something was wrong, they'd dressed and ridden as fast as they could.

"Father would have come, too," Maggie told them, "but—"

"I understand, Maggie," Cleve said quickly. Everyone knew that Maggie's father hadn't been himself since the end of the Civil War, which was why Maggie, with Buck to love and help her, was in charge of the ranch.

Maggie's hand flashed through the pale dawn air as she swept back her copper-colored hair, a gesture that meant she was thinking about something. "What's on your mind?" Buck asked, moving close to her and lowering his voice.

Maggie's eyes went from Teyah, who had just come down from the house, to Charlotte. Teyah's dress was crisp and clean, while Charlotte's was gray with soot and smoke. "Charlotte helped put out the fire," Maggie said with a sense of astonishment.

"So?" Buck shrugged his shoulders.

Maggie tried to explain it to him. "Charlotte would rather *die* then get dirt under her fingernails, at least the Charlotte I know. Just look at her, Buck. What came over her, I wonder?"

Maggie didn't get a chance to say more because, at that moment, Juan Ortiz and his father came riding up. Like Buck and Maggie, they'd seen the firelight on the horizon and come to help.

Charlotte knew it was Juan Ortiz even before she turned around. She didn't know how she knew, she just *knew*. Suddenly there he was, smiling as he dismounted and walked toward her.

"Good morning, Senorita Harmon," he said. Even at this early hour he was dressed in the dashing black shirt and pants of a vaquero.

The way he looked at her as he spoke made Charlotte suddenly aware of her ruined dress and tangled hair. More than anything it made her aware of the scandalous fact that she wasn't wearing a single petticoat. She wondered if he could tell.

"You are up very early, I see," Juan added, his eyes skimming boldly over her.

Charlotte felt a spark of electricity fly between them as she returned his glance. *I wonder if he feels it too*, she thought. Rising to the challenge, she forced herself not to reveal the excitement she felt. She replied as calmly as if she were seated in her own parlor. "The fire woke everyone. Even the smaller ranchers came to help, I see."

As Charlotte said this, she nodded toward several other neighbors who'd just ridden up. But both she and Juan knew that the remark had been meant to put him in his place. La Jota, built on the land his father had obtained from Maggie McNeill, wasn't nearly as large as Cielo Hermoso.

But Juan, to Charlotte's consternation, didn't seem at all wounded by her comment. "There's just one thing I must tell you," he said, a gleam in his dark eyes.

"What?" Charlotte responded, unable to suppress her curiosity.

"Your nose. There is a rather large streak of soot right across it."

"Oh!" Charlotte's cheeks reddened as she lifted her hand to wipe the soot away.

Juan caught her hand in midair. Charlotte was surprised at the strength she felt coursing from his body into hers.

"No, no, leave it." He smiled, a dazzling smile, white teeth flashing. "I like it. It is *encantador*."

"*Encantador?*" Charlotte echoed, not recognizing the Spanish word.

"*Sí, encantador*. Enchanting."

Charlotte couldn't help herself. She smiled back at Juan. And left the spot of soot exactly where it was.

Although the fire was nearly out, there was still much work to be done, work that Buck and Juan and Juan's father and the others who'd come helped with. They continued to douse water over the smoldering debris, making sure that the blaze would not flare up again. Then Juan and his father, both of whom were expert with horses, looked at the animals that had been brought out of the burning stables.

"Burns like this one," Roberto Ortiz said, running his hands over the tender back of one of the mares, "need special treatment. Wash the wound with milk first, then rub it with a little grease, to protect against insects and the sun."

George Harmon frowned slightly. "How long will it take to heal?"

Roberto Ortiz, who was tall and dark-eyed and dark-haired like his son, shrugged. "It is not easy to say, senor, but none of these horses can be ridden until they are completely healed. That may be several weeks."

"I understand," said George Harmon, his frown deepening. Now that the shock and danger had passed, he was beginning to calculate how much money he had lost.

Charlotte turned to Juan, who happened to be standing at her elbow. "Will you look at Lisette for me?" she asked, and without waiting for his answer, she began calling to the little horse. Lisette, however, would not come when Charlotte called her.

"Well!" exclaimed Charlotte indignantly. "I saved her life not more than two hours ago, and now she doesn't want anything to do with me! You'd think she'd be at least a *little* grateful!"

Juan laughed. Charlotte Harmon had a reputation for being beautiful but difficult, not unlike the filly that pranced at the opposite end of the paddock. Yet it was the difficult part of her, as much as her beauty, that he responded to. He knew that she looked down on him because he wasn't wealthy, and the realization piqued his pride. *Someday,* he thought to himself, *I will show her that I am more than that—much more!*

"Lisette! Oh, *Lisette!*" she cried in disgust.

"Is that Lisette?" Juan questioned. "The one with the white stockings and white star, there, over by the fence?"

Charlotte nodded.

With one smooth movement Juan climbed the paddock fence. The horses did not snort and start away from him, as horses sometimes did when a stranger came among them, but accepted his presence. He moved through them to Lisette, who, shamelessly, Charlotte saw, stretched her neck up for him to scratch.

"So this is your Lisette?" he called back with a wide grin. "I think she'll live."

There was no mistaking the arrogance in his voice, Charlotte thought; no mistaking the implication that he knew more about horses than she would ever know. If she hadn't been so relieved to see Lisette acting normally, she would have put him in his place the way he deserved to be put in his place. It was something she was very good at. Maybe Juan knew how to handle horses, but *she* knew how to handle Juan and people like him. At least that's what she told herself as he came striding back across the paddock to her.

"There is nothing at all wrong with your horse, senorita," he told her, "except, perhaps, that she has not been properly trained."

Juan wasn't certain why he enjoyed seeing the anger that flashed so suddenly in Charlotte Harmon's green eyes, but he did.

"I suppose things would be entirely different if Lisette were your horse," Charlotte retorted.

Juan gave her a knowing smile.

It angered her even more that he didn't reply, though his meaning was clear enough. He was telling her that of course Lisette would be better trained if she were a La Jota horse.

As Juan watched, enjoying her frustration, Charlotte's face grew suddenly ashen. "What is it, senorita?" he asked.

Charlotte didn't notice the true concern showing on his face. She was stricken by the words she had just overheard behind her, words spoken by her father to Juan's father. George Harmon had just asked Roberto Ortiz if he was interested in buying any of the horses in the paddock before them.

"Perhaps," Roberto Ortiz replied, and though his words were noncommittal, Charlotte heard the clear interest in his voice.

Shaking off her shock, she turned to the two men. "You're not going to sell our horses, Papa?" she asked, her voice so stiff with alarm that everyone turned to look at her.

"This is business, Charlotte," George Harmon said firmly. There was a certain warning note in his voice, a warning note that Charlotte chose to ignore.

"But what are you thinking of?" she persisted. "These are *our* horses."

George Harmon's flinty gray eyes met his daughter's icy green ones. "We don't have a place to keep them anymore," he said, gesturing toward the ruined stable.

Charlotte tossed her head impatiently. "Not right now, no, but we'll rebuild."

"Yes," her father replied slowly, "but I'm thinking of putting up a smaller stable. The hands keep their own horses out on the range and so a stable . . . well, we've always kept more riding horses than we needed, and it's become a great expense. We'll keep Minx and Lisette and the other family horses, of course," he added quickly.

He tried to end on a placating note, but Charlotte was having none of it. The Cielo Hermoso horses mattered a great deal to her. They were part of her world, something that belonged to her. She wasn't about to have them whisked away from her.

"I don't believe what you're saying, Papa," she gasped in astonishment. Watching her, Juan Ortiz saw the firm set of her jaw and knew that

George Harmon was in for a fight. It would have surprised her to know that he understood, at that moment, exactly what she was feeling. When something was yours, you fought for it. It was as simple as that.

George Harmon cleared his throat. "But, Charlotte—"

Charlotte interrupted her father, an idea swiftly taking shape in her mind. "Don't you see what an opportunity this is, Papa?" she asked.

"What do you mean?" her father asked.

"Everyone's always said our horses are the best in Texas, so why not take advantage of it? Why not breed horses and sell them? As a business, I mean. We ought to build a bigger stable, not a smaller one."

"What you're talking about is a lot of work, Charlotte. My hands are already full with the cattle and the cotton."

Charlotte continued. "If you're not interested in starting a horse business, I am. I'll see to everything myself." She paused, her heart beating rapidly. Each word out of her mouth surprised her more than the one before it. "Cielo Hermoso will be mine someday. Part of it, anyway," she added, glancing at Teyah and Cleve. "So let me start taking care of it now. Please, Papa."

"Now, Charlotte," her father replied soothingly. He'd spoiled her too much, he saw, given her her own way too many times. "This isn't a game, you know," he said, shifting his tone of voice. "This is serious."

Charlotte shifted with him. Suddenly the child before George Harmon vanished; in her place stood a determined young woman. "I know it's serious, Papa." She hesitated just a moment. "I'll be responsible for everything."

In the moment of silence that followed, Charlotte felt a spark of fear glowing inside her. What was she doing, taking on this enormous responsibility? But something else inside her would not let the idea go. Cielo Hermoso's stable must stand again, and it must stand even grander than before. Beside the spark of fear a spark of excitement fanned into existence. She pictured not one stable but several, long, white-painted buildings with glossy green trim. She overheard, in her mind, people saying, "There're no stables in Texas that can match Cielo Hermoso's. It's all Charlotte Harmon's doing, you know, and they say she's made millions."

Looking straight at her father, Charlotte repeated the words she'd said before, but this time with more conviction. "I'll be responsible for everything, Papa."

He looked at her, debating whether or not to let her have her chance. He was about to say no when suddenly a memory came to him, a memory of himself as a young man struggling to establish Cielo Hermoso. It had been the best experience of his life. Didn't Charlotte deserve the same kind of chance? Even if she failed, she was bound to learn from it. Perhaps, he thought with a wry smile, she would even grow up along the way.

"If you're determined to do this, Charlotte, I'll give you the money you need. But I'm warning you, no giving up in the middle or quitting and expecting me to take over. I won't. If you don't go through with it, I'll tear down the stable, however far you've gotten, and cut back our stock just as I planned. Whatever money is lost will come out of your share of Cielo Hermoso. Do you understand?"

"I understand," she answered with a swift, firm nod.

George Harmon cleared his throat. He hadn't thought she'd agree to his challenge, so he tried another approach. "You can't do the work yourself," he said. "Who are you going to get to help you?"

Charlotte hadn't thought that far ahead. Now, looking across the paddock, she saw Cleve. "Cleve will help. Won't you, Cleve?" she called brightly, and smiled when he replied with an unhesitating nod.

"That's fine," George Harmon said. "But Cleve alone isn't enough, and he doesn't know much about building. Who're you going to hire to take charge of things?"

Suddenly Charlotte feared that her father was about to say no to her after all. Turning, she saw Juan Ortiz. *He* knew how to build things, she thought. With his father he had built the house at La Jota as well as the barn and stable and outbuildings.

"Juan," she said impulsively, desperate to answer her father's question.

"Juan has his own place, La Jota, to worry about."

"But winter's coming," Charlotte argued. "There's never much work on a ranch in the wintertime. And I'll give him a share in the profits."

"What profits," asked George Harmon, momentarily distracted.

"There'll be profits," Charlotte said with conviction. "Maybe not right away, but I intend to make a fortune!"

George Harmon clicked his tongue against his teeth. He'd meant for his daughter to see how difficult the task she proposed was going to be. Instead she'd leaped ahead of him with grand plans of her own. "You don't know the first thing about horses," he pointed out.

"Juan does," Charlotte answered. "So if he agrees to help me, not just with the stables but with the horses too—" She was getting ahead of herself and she knew it. When her father interrupted her with a wave of his hand, she was almost relieved.

"How do you know Juan's even interested?" George Harmon asked.

That was the flaw in the plan, the flaw Charlotte had hoped wouldn't come to light. That was why she hadn't addressed Juan himself or even dared look him in the eye. Why would Juan be interested in working with her, Juan who was so proud and whom she kept trying to put out of her mind?

Never in a million years did Charlotte expect what happened next. She never expected Juan to step forward and say, in a voice so masculine and serious that it sent a shiver up her spine, "You are wrong, Senor Harmon. I would be most interested in your daughter's offer."

Chapter Three

Charlotte wasn't certain that Juan would live up to his part of the bargain.

"What if he's just trying to make me look like a fool?" she asked Teyah anxiously. "What if he's going to leave me stranded with lumber and a crew and no one in charge?"

Teyah shook her head. "If Juan gave his word, he'll be here. You have to trust him."

Reluctantly Charlotte agreed. She had no choice. She had to trust Juan, and so she went ahead and ordered lumber and hired a work crew. Even so, she was as surprised as anyone to wake one morning to the sound of Juan's voice in the yard. Hastily, embarrassed to have slept late, she dressed and rushed downstairs. Only when she was standing in the yard, peering at Juan through the bluish dawn, did she realize that she hadn't overslept at all. Why, it can't be more than five A.M.! she thought.

"You will have to start getting up earlier, senorita," Juan told her. "My men cannot work without breakfast."

That was their agreement, that he would direct the men and the building while she would be in charge of getting the meals. She looked at him carefully, certain that he was teasing her, certain that she would see his usual faintly mocking smile. But Juan was perfectly serious.

"What time is it?" she asked.

"Nearly five," he answered. "My men will expect breakfast at four-thirty."

Charlotte swallowed. She had seen the hour of four-thirty once or twice in her life, but always from the other end, coming home from a ball or staying up late to read a romantic novel. But never, *ever*, had anyone suggested that she rise at such an hour. To have breakfast ready for the crew by then, she would have to get up at three.

"Is that acceptable to you?" Juan asked. The look on his face said that it would have to be, and after thinking about it, Charlotte understood why. The more hours of daylight that were wasted, the longer it would take to build the stables and the more it would cost.

"Certainly," she said. "I won't oversleep again. Tell the men I'm sorry and I'll send something out to them as soon as I can get it ready."

She returned to the house, wanting desperately to yawn but afraid to in case Juan was watching her. He was, in fact, watching her, watching her and experiencing a profound sense of relief. For just as she had distrusted him, he had distrusted her.

"Charlotte Harmon is a rich, spoiled girl," his father had warned him. "She will give the whole idea up as soon as she sees that real work is required. The whole thing is crazy, loco."

Although he feared that his father was right, Juan would not back down. He defended Charlotte, in fact, knowing that he would look all the more foolish if she reneged on their bargain.

Now, watching her move across the yard toward the house, he knew that things would work out between them. There would be stormy moments, to be sure, but they would only add some spice to the arrangement.

One of those moments came just two days later. Charlotte had drawn a sketch of the stables, three long white buildings running parallel to each other, connected by elaborate arches over which, she imagined, beautiful grape arbors would grow. But when the foundations were laid, she saw that the three buildings were being arranged in a giant U.

"What's going on here?" she asked Cleve. "Was this your idea?"

Her eyes snapped with such fire that, for a moment, Cleve considered saying that it was his idea, just to avoid the explosive argument that was bound to take place between Charlotte and Juan. His sense of honesty won out, however, and he told her the truth. "It was Juan's idea," he answered, "but I agreed with him."

Charlotte didn't hear the last part of his statement. Whirling away from him, she marched to where Juan was directing the workmen. Hitching her skirts up, she climbed over the knee-high wall that was already being hammered into place, no longer paying attention to whether or not her ankles were exposed. "You changed my plans," she said accusingly. Instantly hammers came to a halt in midair.

"*Our* plans, I believe," Juan said, turning to her.

"Why?" Her question was as clear and piercing as an icicle in the chilly, sunlit air.

"Because my way is better," Juan replied calmly.

Charlotte's eyes flashed. "What about my arches? What about my grape arbors?"

Juan sighed. "Charlotte, have you ever seen such arbors in Texas?"

"No."

"That is because grapevines do not grow in this soil. Has that never occurred to you?"

It had crossed Charlotte's mind once, but she assumed that if given enough time and attention, grapevines could grow at Cielo Hermoso. "If I want grape arbors," she said, "I will have grape arbors."

Juan remained calm. "And block out sun and air between the stables? Those are the very things horses need, not grape leaves."

One of the hands chuckled, but a look from Charlotte swiftly silenced him. "Why have you changed the arrangement?" she asked, letting go, for the moment, of the grape arbors.

"Because this way is better. Come here, I will show you." Charlotte hesitated. "Come here, come here," he repeated, smiling now. Drawing her forward, he led her to the middle of the U-shaped space. "See how this forms a natural paddock?" he questioned. "When buyers come, they can view every stall from here." Putting his hands lightly on her shoulders, he turned her toward each of the three buildings. Charlotte ignored the spark of excitement that accompanied his touch. "And from here," Juan continued, turning her back to face the center space, "a horse may be walked and shown. Most impressive, don't you agree?"

"But—"

"The best, the wealthiest, ranches in Mexico are built this way, even El Rancho de las Fuentes."

Charlotte, who'd been readying an argument, fell silent for a moment. "El Rancho de las Fuentes?" she echoed.

"*Sí.*"

Though it was far to the south, below the Mexican border, every Texan who knew and loved horses was familiar with El Rancho de las Fuentes and its fine, hot-blooded mounts. It was exactly the kind of reputation that she wanted for Cielo Hermoso.

"Well," Charlotte said at last, relenting but not wanting to lose face, "I *had* thought of a U-shaped arrangement, but I know it's more difficult to lay out. I wasn't sure you could handle it."

"We will handle it, senorita."

"If you're sure you can." She smiled, a dimple appearing on each side of her face.

Juan was entranced. "Of course I am sure. You have nothing to worry about," he assured her.

Charlotte's dimples deepened. "Don't I?"

The question hung between them like a bubble, a bubble that burst only when Juan said he must get back to work.

Never again, after that first morning, did Juan arrive to find Charlotte still asleep. Motivated by pride and willpower, she got herself out of bed and down to the kitchen by three-thirty every morning. There she would begin directing Flora, Nina, and the other servants in the making of breakfast. By the time the men arrived, there would be hot corn bread, fried potatoes, and grilled steak waiting for them. As soon as the meal was over, the cycle began all over again, for an even bigger lunch would be demanded by the hungry men.

The crew ate at a long, oilcloth-covered table positioned in the backyard just outside the kitchen door. Supervising the cooking and lugging plates and platters back and forth took an enormous amount of Charlotte's energy. So did running back and forth to the stable site and interfering with Juan's handling of the crew. One day, after an especially spirited argument over how deep the hayracks were to be, Juan looked at her in puzzled awe.

"Don't you ever get tired, senorita?" he asked.

Charlotte shook her head. "Not in the least. Do you?"

"Of course not," Juan answered swiftly. "An Ortiz does not know the meaning of the word."

They were both lying, of course. Juan had recently discovered that directing men was much more difficult than directing cattle, while Charlotte, who had never expected to work a day in her life, tumbled into bed almost as soon as dinner was over. She'd been sound asleep the night Billy Joe Briscoe and his father left and, in the days since then, had missed two parties because, as she told her maid, Luz, she was too tired to stand up while her stays were laced.

"I don't understand," Teyah said one afternoon as they cut the corn bread, just out of the oven, into large squares.

"Understand what?" Charlotte asked.

"You," Teyah answered.

Once, Charlotte would have bristled defensively at the remark. It had taken her months to get used to Teyah. Sometimes she wasn't sure she was quite used to her yet. But things had gotten better between them lately. Maybe it was because Teyah, without needing to be asked, got up each morning with Charlotte to help her cook for the men. Or maybe it was because, as Maggie McNeill suspected, Teyah was safely in love with Cleve and no longer a threat to Charlotte where young men were concerned. Whatever the reasons, Charlotte didn't stop to examine them. She didn't have the time.

"Why don't you understand me?" she asked, wrapping a towel around the handle of a cast-iron stewpot and lifting it from the stove.

"You missed two parties this week," Teyah said. "Aren't you just *miserable*?"

Charlotte laughed. Teyah, who'd learned much of her English at Cielo Hermoso, said "just *miserable*" exactly the way Charlotte usually said it, with a high-pitched squeal of despair. "I don't have time to think about it, I guess," she answered at last, lugging the stewpot toward the door.

"Does that mean you're happy?" Teyah asked, not wanting to let the topic go. Now that she'd fallen in love with Cleve, she was anxious for everyone else to be as happy as she was.

"I don't know," Charlotte answered, bumping open the door with her hip.

Inside she was thinking that there had to be more to happiness than dreaming of a full night's sleep. But if she said that to Teyah, Teyah would start talking about Cleve and about being in love and how wonderful it all was. Not that Charlotte disbelieved her. Love was wonderful. It must be if everyone kept telling her so. The only thing was, she'd never been in love herself, and the only men who ever seemed to love her were the Billy Joe Briscoes of the world. When Teyah or Maggie talked about love and about the special, glowing feeling it gave them, Charlotte felt left out. She thought again of how unfair it was that she, Charlotte Harmon, had never been kissed by anybody she *really* liked.

Pushing the thought from her mind, Charlotte stepped swiftly across the porch with the heavy stewpot. Three steep stairs led down to the yard and the oilcloth covered table. As she started down them, Charlotte felt her foot just miss the first step.

Inside, Teyah heard a cry and came running to help. Somehow, miraculously, Charlotte had managed to fall without spilling the food.

"Are you all right?" Teyah asked.

Charlotte bit her lip and blinked back tears of pain. Her effort to save the food had had a high price, for the calf of her leg had been burned against the side of the hot kettle. Turning back her skirt, she showed Teyah the angry red mark.

"I'll get help," Teyah said, running instinctively for Cleve.

But it was Juan who was the first one up from the site. "I hear you attacked the stewpot," he said with a slight smile. But when he saw the red welt, his smile vanished.

"It hurts," Charlotte said. She didn't want to cry, especially in front of him, but she couldn't help it. The pain was getting worse with each second that passed.

Without another word, without even asking her permission, Juan picked her up and carried her back into the kitchen. "Out, out, out," he shouted to Flora and Nina, who came crowding to see what the matter was. "The men are coming up to eat, go help Teyah with the food." Flora and Nina didn't budge. "Go, I said."

Charlotte, between waves of pain, managed to explain what the trouble was. "It's not their job," she said. "They are cooks, not maids. They will not serve food. Let me down, I have to do it, somehow."

She felt Juan's arms tighten around her. "Ridiculous!" he exclaimed. "Go," he repeated sternly, glowering at the two women. *"Vayanse!"*

Flora, the older of the two, looked squarely at Juan and fired a string of Spanish words at him. Instantly color rose to Juan's cheeks.

"What did she say?" Charlotte asked, curious in spite of her pain.

"They will not leave me alone with you. They do not seem to think it is proper."

Charlotte's laughter startled the two women. "Go," she said. "It's all right. Truly."

Reluctantly Flora and Nina went outside to help Teyah.

"Now," Juan said, still embarrassed over the cooks' lack of trust, "we'll take care of your burn."

He set her down on the table and pumped cold water at the sink, saturating a towel with it.

"I can manage now," Charlotte said, trying to take the towel from him.

"I don't think so," he replied firmly. "Your leg, please."

"What?" Revealing one's leg to a young man, even in these circumstances, was not at all the usual thing.

"Your leg," Juan repeated.

Charlotte, returning to herself, clicked her tongue against her teeth. "This is most improper," she said.

Behind Juan's look of concern was the unmistakable ghost of a smile. "I know," he said. Lifting her skirt and petticoats just to the knee, Charlotte stretched out her leg and let Juan wrap the cold towel around the burn. Instantly the pain began to subside.

"Does that feel better, senorita?" he asked.

"Yes," Charlotte answered. Juan's hands, inspecting the burn, were long-fingered and gentle. She found herself wondering if those hands had ever reached around a girl's waist or run excitedly through someone's hair.

"You are so silent," he said suddenly. "What are you thinking?"

Charlotte took a quick breath. "I am thinking that milk is what you're supposed to put on burns, not water. At least that's what your father said about our horses after the stable fire."

Juan smiled slightly. "You, senorita, are decidedly not a horse."

He was standing very close to her, so close she could see a vein in his neck pulsing. *His eyes aren't black at all*, she thought with surprise, looking directly into them; *they're dark brown, dark brown like coffee. They only look black until you get close.*

"You're missing your lunch," she said.

"I don't mind."

He leaned closer to her, a gesture she knew from Billy Joe Briscoe and all the other boys in her life. Instead of pulling away, as she could have

done so easily, she sat just where she was. And
waited. The waiting seemed to go on forever.

Suddenly there came the sound of boots in
the hallway. "So here you are," her father said,
entering the room. "I heard that you got hurt."

"A burn," Juan explained. "Your daughter
will be all right."

A look passed from George Harmon to the
young man, but Charlotte, lost in her own
confusion, missed it. What was happening to
her? Had Juan been about to kiss her or had she
only imagined it? Her whole body tingled, not
just the burn on her leg but her cheeks and her
lips and even the palms of her hands.

It was a feeling she wasn't sure she liked at
all. She was used to being in control, in charge of
things, and that wasn't the case where Juan was
concerned. Even so, as she lay in bed that night,
she closed her eyes and tried to bring back that
tingling, exciting feeling and, with it, Juan's smile
and voice and the sense of his nearness.

Chapter Four

Charlotte's burn healed quickly and, just as quickly, the stables took shape. One evening, after the day's work was finished, Charlotte went alone to inspect the almost-finished buildings. Winter sunlight splashed against the stalls, and the smell of new lumber filled the cool air. Moving down the row of stalls, Charlotte could imagine them filled with mares and their foals. The best stall of all, she decided, would be for Lisette.

A noise attracted her attention. Charlotte tensed. She was alone, completely unprotected, and the sounds coming from the stall ahead of her were definitely human. "Who's there?" she called, and without waiting for an answer, plunged boldly forward. Suddenly a man rose up before her. "Juan!"

"*Sí*. I didn't frighten you, did I?"

"Of course not." She paused, realizing that it was the first time they'd been alone together since the day he'd soothed her burn. "What are you doing here?" she demanded.

"Perhaps I am looking for you, senorita," he replied with a smile. "That is what you were thinking, no?"

It was *exactly* what she was thinking, but she was horrified to have him know it. "I have better things to think about," she replied tartly.

"Perhaps, perhaps not," Juan answered, enjoying her discomfort. Watching a blush come to her cheeks was extremely satisfying, as was watching the way she tossed her mane of golden hair.

"You never did tell me," she said, "what you're doing here."

"I'm your partner, remember?"

"Oh, yes, I'd nearly forgotten."

He chuckled, enjoying her crisp sarcasm. "I was fixing the door," he told her. "The door to this stable. See? It did not hang right." Pointing to the lower half of the double door, he showed her where he'd planed the wood away.

Charlotte drew near him. She gave the door a push and watched as it swung shut, a perfect fit.

"You approve of my work, I take it?" he asked, looking at her boldly.

There was more to the question than words alone and they both knew it. Suddenly, fearing that the situation was about to slip beyond her control, Charlotte resorted to a ploy she'd used with other boys.

"Whatever do you mean?" she asked, casting her glance demurely down.

But Juan was not like the other boys she'd known. When Charlotte looked up, he was still looking at her.

"I think you do know what I mean, Charlotte," he said.

Juan, like Charlotte, was experiencing feelings he'd never had before. There had been girls in his life, yes, but never a girl like this one. He wanted to take her in his arms, to show her that he was better than the soft young men she was used to. He wouldn't do it, though. Not as long as she was acting like a spoiled flirt.

"No, I *don't* know what you mean," she insisted stubbornly. Then she turned, expecting him to come after her, to take her in his arms and show her what it was that they'd been talking about. When he didn't do that, she felt a wave of confusion mixed with anger. Was he toying with her? Had she misread the look in his eyes? Never in her life had Charlotte felt on such shaky footing.

"You never told me," Juan said, coming up behind her, "what you're doing here."

"I'm your partner, remember?" she replied tartly, echoing his words of a moment ago.

Juan laughed. Then, suddenly, his face grew serious. He was even more handsome, Charlotte thought, when he wasn't joking. His face, with its high cheekbones and broad, firm mouth, seemed chiseled from sandstone. His eyes swept the nearly completed buildings, then came to rest on her. "These will be fine stables," he said at last.

Charlotte's eyes glistened with excitement. "Yes, they will, won't they?"

Juan gave her a gentle smile. "Why don't you do that more often?" he asked.

"Do what?"

"Be yourself. You are quite likable, you know, when you are not playing games."

Charlotte stiffened. She felt vulnerable, as transparent as a piece of glass. "You call them games," she said, "others call them manners, something you, obviously, don't know anything about."

She turned away from him and began marching back the way she had come, past the long row of empty stalls. She had not gone more than ten paces when she felt Juan's hand on her shoulder.

He spun her around, so suddenly and so forcefully that she gasped in surprise. Their eyes met and held and, in that moment, they were totally honest with each other. There were no games and no defenses. There were only strong and undeniable feelings for each other.

Charlotte felt herself move forward and felt Juan's lips on hers. It was like a wave rolling up to the shore, she thought; a wave that carried you right along with it.

How many times had she been kissed? Fifty? One hundred? It didn't matter, because none of them had felt like this.

Finally, frightened by the intensity of her own feelings, Charlotte pulled away. Without a word she hurried toward the house, both relieved and disappointed that, this time, Juan didn't try to follow her.

Juan lay half-asleep, smiling in the predawn stillness as he thought of Charlotte. He was remembering yesterday, remembering the passionate way she'd kissed him and the equally passionate way she'd drawn away. A girl as unpredictable as a whirlwind, he thought, wondering what the day ahead would bring. Would she be eager to pick up where they'd left off, or would she act as if the kiss had never happened?

The sudden snorting of a horse interrupted his thoughts and pulled his nerves taut. In the darkness of the small house he looked toward his father's bed and saw a shadowy movement.

"I hear them," Roberto Ortiz said softly, rising.

Juan nodded and reached, in the darkness, for his clothes and his gun.

Two days ago four head of cattle had been rustled from La Jota. Since then both Juan and his father had expected the thieves to return.

"I'm going after them," Juan said.

"Alone? No. It is too dangerous. We don't know how many of them there are. I will come too."

Now it was Juan's turn to shake his head. "And leave La Jota unprotected? No, let me go alone. I'll stay hidden from them, and if I have an opportunity to get our cattle back, I will. If not, at least I can find out who they are." There was a long silence while Roberto Ortiz considered the possibilities. "We must do *something*, Father," Juan added urgently.

Roberto Ortiz nodded. It was true. Whoever was stealing their cattle would go right on rustling until they themselves put a stop to it. Unlike the larger ranchers in the area, the Ortizes could not afford to hire hands. Their cattle grazed unprotected, easy prey for the thieves.

"I'm going to go, then," Juan said.

His father looked at him. "What about your work at Cielo Hermoso?"

"They will work for a day without me."

"But shouldn't you send word somehow? Explain where you've gone?"

Juan shook his head vehemently. If Charlotte knew about the rustlers, she would pity him, a small rancher who couldn't guard his own cattle. She might even go to her father and ask him to help. Juan shuddered at the thought, his pride bristling. "This is our problem, Father," he said firmly, "and we will take care of it. No one else needs to know."

Roberto Ortiz nodded. When it came to matters of pride, his son was exactly like him.

Juan trailed the rustlers all day, taking care to keep well out of sight. There were three of them, too many to challenge, driving ten La Jota cattle before them. As soon as they were out of the area, Juan knew, they would change the La Jota brand by covering it with another mark. Then, claiming the cattle as their own, they would sell them to some unsuspecting rancher. Juan's blood boiled with anger as he rode along. Not these cattle, he told himself. The rustlers were in for a surprise.

He waited until sundown, when the rustlers settled down for the night. As soon as he was certain the three men were asleep, he slipped into the camp. The cattle, grazing in the moonlight, were not difficult to gather together. Nor were the rustlers' horses. When he'd gathered all the animals together, Juan pointed his gun in the air and fired a single shot, a shot that sent both the cattle and the rustlers' horses running swiftly across the prairie.

Juan grinned as he herded the cattle and guided them back toward La Jota. The rustlers were wide awake now, but little good it would do them. Without their horses they were helpless. And the cattle, Juan thought with satisfaction, were once again the property of La Jota.

He rode all through the night and reached home just before dawn. He had ridden nearly twenty-four hours without food or rest and longed, more than anything, for slumber. But slumber was out of the question. He had missed one day's work at Cielo Hermoso; he could not afford to miss another.

"Did Charlotte come looking for me yesterday?" he asked his father as he splashed water onto his face and changed quickly into fresh clothing.

"No," Roberto Ortiz replied, "but someone else did."

"Who?" Juan asked.

"Rose Fontaine."

Juan lifted his eyebrows. He had never heard the name before.

"She said her family is new in the area," Juan's father explained. "She wishes to hire you to do some work, the same kind of work you are doing at Cielo Hermoso."

"I wonder where she heard of me," Juan mused. Then, shrugging, he said, "At any rate, she was misinformed. Cielo Hermoso is a challenging project, but I have no wish to go into the building business. If Senora Fontaine returns, tell her I'm not interested."

"Not senora," Roberto Ortiz said, a faint smile lighting his eyes. "Senorita. Very young, very pretty, and very determined to have her own way. I'm not sure she'll take no for an answer."

"She'll have to," Juan replied. Without giving Rose Fontaine another thought, he turned toward Cielo Hermoso and Charlotte.

Like Juan, Charlotte hadn't slept the night before, but she hadn't slept for a very different reason: She was thinking of him. Juan's failure to show up for work had left her stunned. What had happened? Was he sick? Injured? Or had he decided that, having kissed her, he wanted nothing more to do with her?

Never before had Charlotte let herself go as she had with Juan. Never had she surrendered control as she had with him. And now that she had, she needed his presence and his reassurance. Instead his absence left her feeling puzzled and confused. *He must be ill*, she'd told herself as she'd tossed and turned, waiting for sleep that wouldn't come. *Tomorrow, I'll go to him.*

The next morning, just as she was preparing to ride to La Jota, she saw Juan's horse entering the yard. Even from a distance, even though it was not quite sunup, she could see that he wasn't sick. Nothing at all was wrong with him. He'd stayed away simply because he'd felt like it! The realization stung Charlotte. Anger surged forward, covering over her hurt feelings.

One kiss, she thought, *one little kiss and he thinks he can do anything he likes! Why, he doesn't care about me at all—he's just interested in making things easy for himself.*

She blushed to think that she'd been used so easily and blushed even more to think that, only a few hours ago, she'd been half in love with Juan. *Well, we'll just see about that*, she told herself, staring at him as he dismounted.

"Good morning," Juan called, determined to hide all traces of his exhaustion from her.

If Charlotte had paused a moment, she would have seen the dark circles beneath his eyes and the tired look on his face. But she didn't pause. She whirled down off the steps like a tornado. "Where were you yesterday?" she demanded.

"Business," he replied. "I couldn't come."

Charlotte waited for him to say more. Didn't he understand that you didn't just kiss someone and then disappear? Not if the kiss was important to you, anyway.

"What kind of business?" she persisted, still hoping for an explanation.

For a moment he considered explaining everything, telling her about the rustlers and about his ride to recapture his cattle. Part of him wanted to tell Charlotte the truth. But another part of him held back. He was proud and stubborn, and most of all he was afraid that she would feel sorry for him. The idea of anyone feeling sorry for him was repugnant to Juan, and the idea of Charlotte feeling sorry for him was especially intolerable.

"What kind of business?" Charlotte asked again.

"*Personal* business," Juan said, and turned away, as if the subject were closed. In his eagerness to conceal the truth his voice was harsher than he'd meant to make it.

Charlotte felt stung. *If he cared about me*, she thought, *if he cared about me at all, he wouldn't shut me out this way*. Never in her life had she felt so rejected. Anger bubbled up inside her, forming itself into words that escaped before she could stop them.

"You're fired!" she cried.

Juan turned to face her. "What?" He didn't quite believe what he'd just heard.

Charlotte felt shaky, as surprised at her words as he was, but she would not back down. "Maybe you don't think I can manage without you," she snapped.

"Can you?" Juan asked.

He was talking about more than work and they both knew it. The memory of the kiss flashed in both their minds.

"I certainly *can* manage without you," Charlotte retorted. "So if you can't be here when you're supposed to be, consider yourself fired."

Her words hit a nerve in Juan. So nothing had changed between them after all—she thought of him as nothing more than a hired hand!

"Very well, senorita," he said softly, a muscle in his jaw working. "Whatever you wish."

Charlotte didn't believe that Juan would actually get on his horse and ride away, but he did. "Good!" she shouted angrily, bounding after his retreating form. "I'll finish my stables without you! Wait and see!"

Even before the dust of his horse's hooves had settled, Charlotte began to suspect that she'd made a mistake. She hated Juan, she told herself; she hated his indifference to her. But now that he was gone, she felt as if something important had been taken away.

Angry and confused, she walked back into the kitchen. A stack of plain white china plates sat on the counter. Her hand went to the top plate, lifted it, and hurled it to the floor. The sound of breaking china was so satisfying that she smashed a second plate as well.

Alarmed at the sound, Nina came hurrying into the room. In one swift glance Nina took in the broken dishes, Juan's absence, and the look on Charlotte's face. "Ah," she said, *"amor."*

Charlotte didn't speak Spanish but she knew what *amor* meant. "No, no, no!" she cried furiously. "I don't love him at all. Not at all!" And, for good measure, she sent a third plate crashing to the floor.

Chapter Five

Finishing the stables wasn't as easy as Charlotte had thought it would be. The crew, angry because they felt that Juan had been unfairly fired, viewed her with suspicion. They even went so far, Charlotte suspected, as to refuse to follow her orders.

"Why didn't you put that door where I told you to?" she raged one day.

"Because you told me to put it in the wrong place, that's why," Luke Hanks raged back at her.

"Here, now," Cleve said, hearing the raised voices and hurrying over to them. "What's the trouble?"

"He's ruining my stables!" Charlotte cried. "He's spoiling everything!"

Cleve's brown eyes looked soberly at Hanks. "Is that true, Luke?"

"Tarnation, no," the hand replied. "She doesn't know what she's talking about, that's all."

Charlotte's green eyes flashed. "I do so know what I'm talking about, and I know the door goes right over there!"

"Where are the plans?" Cleve asked, turning to her. "Do you have them or did Juan take them with him?"

At the mention of Juan's name Charlotte tossed her head. "I still have them," she said, and hurried off to get them.

She was certain that the plans would prove her right. And at first they seemed to. But when Cleve took the papers from her and turned them right side up, she saw that she'd been looking at them upside down.

"Well, that's always the way Juan held them," she protested.

"Of course it was."

Charlotte thought she detected an amused sparkle in Cleve's eye. "Well, it was!"

Cleve patted her shoulder. "Simmer down, Charlotte. You're just tired and overworked. Anyone can make a mistake."

Charlotte's head jerked so sharply that her chin almost struck Cleve's shoulder. "I am not at all tired," she informed everyone who was watching her. "Not one little bit."

She *was* tired, of course. She just wouldn't admit it to herself.

The more difficult things became, the harder Charlotte worked to finish the buildings. Her father's words echoed in her mind. *I'm warning you, Charlotte, no giving up in the middle or quitting and expecting me to take over. I won't. If you don't go through with things, I'll tear down the stables, however far you've gotten, and cut back on our riding stock. Whatever money is lost will come out of your share of Cielo Hermoso.*

That couldn't happen, Charlotte thought, her chin falling into a stubborn line, it just couldn't. The thought of Cielo Hermoso as just another cow-and-cotton place was intolerable.

No, Cielo Hermoso, *her* Cielo Hermoso, would have fine stables and beautiful, highly prized horses. And it would have them if she had to hammer every board into place herself!

Charlotte worked twice as hard without Juan as she had with him. In addition to feeding the crew she now took an active part in the building. Long after everyone else had left the site for the day, she would often go back to it, taking advantage of the last daylight to move lumber, sweep up chips and shavings, or sand down stubborn knots in the wood.

The work was exhausting but she welcomed it. Because of it she was always tired, too tired to think about the fact that without Juan nothing was the same. Sometimes she would wake with a start in the middle of the night and wonder what was going to happen after the stables were completed. Juan was to have been her partner in the horse business. Juan was to have helped her decide which horses to breed and told her how to manage them. But she had fired Juan, and he had not, as she had secretly hoped, come begging for his job back.

What are you going to do without him? an inner voice would sometimes ask. Charlotte, to drown out the nagging voice, would pound her pillow in response. *I'll manage to finish the stables somehow,* she told herself; *I don't need Juan Ortiz. Goodness, I can get another partner without any trouble at all.*

But when Charlotte tried to think of who that other partner might be, no names came to mind. Instead she lay awake far into the night, trying to convince herself that she didn't need Juan Ortiz in her life at all.

* * *

Juan was busy in the yard of La Jota mending a worn leather harness. At first, working on his own place again had been a relief to him. At least he would be on hand to defend his ranch if the rustlers came again. But when several days passed without trouble, Juan's thoughts began to wander—back to Cielo Hermoso and back to Charlotte. It was the excitement of building the stables he missed, he told himself; it was the pleasure of watching the structures take shape day by day. But it was more than that and Juan knew it. It was Charlotte herself he missed, her flash and fire. He missed her so much that he even considered riding back to Cielo Hermoso and insisted that he complete work on the stables.

His pride, however, would not let him do so. What if Charlotte shouted him off her land? What if she had him arrested for trespassing? Juan almost smiled at the thought. It was exactly the kind of thing Charlotte might do. Still, he wasn't sure he was ready to expose himself to such extremes of temper. Besides, he decided, it would be good for her to realize how badly she'd behaved. It would be good for her to come to apologize to him.

Juan, hearing hoofbeats as he worked on the harness, looked up eagerly. Cantering toward him was one of the most extraordinary horses he had ever seen. It was pale blond, with a silver white mane and tail and a tooled leather bridle glittering with silver conchos. And seated on the horse, riding with a sense of sureness Juan could not help admiring, was a young woman with hair the color and luster of black glass.

He knew even before she dismounted and introduced herself that it must be Rose Fontaine, the young woman his father had mentioned a few days ago. It was the willful, determined look on her face that gave her away.

"You're Juan, aren't you?" the young woman asked as she slid gracefully from the horse. Her brown eyes sparkled with approval as she looked Juan over from head to toe. "Yes, they said you were handsome. I'm Rose Fontaine. My family has just moved to the county. Or maybe I should say *counties*," she corrected with a smile. "Our ranch runs through three of them."

Rose held out her hand, not thumb up so that he could shake it but palm down so that he could kiss it. Juan, astonished, simply stared at her until, without the least show of embarrassment, she let her hand drop.

"I want to talk to you about doing work for us," Rose said briskly.

"And who might *us* be, senorita?"

"My older brothers and me. We run Belle Monde by ourselves. Our parents are dead."

"I am sorry to hear that," Juan said.

"Don't be," Rose replied. "It happened a long time ago. I don't even remember them, to tell you the truth. And being an orphan has left me very rich."

Her words jolted Juan. He had never heard anyone talk about the death of their parents so casually. He found himself unconsciously comparing Rose to Charlotte. Charlotte was wealthy and headstrong, too, he thought, but Charlotte had a heart. Her only problem was that she refused to let anyone see it.

Rose was looking curiously at the house. "Goodness," she said, "Our bunkhouses are bigger than this. Do you and your father really live here?"

"*Sí*," Juan answered, stung by her criticism. He was extremely proud of La Jota. He and his father had built it themselves, and that made it more desirable to him than all the other ranches in Texas.

"Do you plan to enlarge it?" Rose persisted.

"It is adequate for my father and me, senorita."

"Perhaps for now," Rose replied, "but one day, well . . ." Her thoughts drifted off. The west Texas plains had at first seemed devoid of any form of interesting male life to her, but now she was beginning to change her mind. She pictured Juan Ortiz dressed in black pants and a white ruffled shirt, standing in the ballroom of Belle Monde as he waited to take her in his arms. That was where he belonged, she decided swiftly, not on this tiny garden plot of a ranch.

"One day what, senorita?" Juan asked.

She could not tell if he was interested or merely annoyed. His brown-black eyes gave her no messages at all. "Wait and see," she said, letting her eyelids flutter mysteriously.

"You say you want to discuss work?" Juan asked impatiently, changing the topic back to something he was more comfortable with.

"Yes. Maybe your father told you. I want you to hire a crew to build another stable for us. I've heard you did wonders at Cielo Hermoso, given the difficult circumstances."

Juan could not help smiling. News of Charlotte's temper certainly spread fast!

"Now, then," Rose said, "let's discuss terms."

"One moment, senorita," Juan said.

"Whatever you were earning at Cielo Hermoso," Rose said temptingly, "I will double it."

Juan considered. With so much money he and his father could add to their cattle stock. "May I think about it?" he asked at last, unwilling to accept the offer and become, in every sense of the word, Rose Fontaine's hired hand.

Rose smiled, certain that Juan would see things her way if she gave him time. "Of course," she said. "And I have the perfect way for you to give me your answer."

"What is that?"

"Come to my ball next Friday," she said. "You can tell me then that you accept."

"I will tell you then *whether* I accept," Juan corrected.

"*That* you accept," Rose finished, insistent upon having the last word. She remounted her horse. "I will see you next Friday," she called, and shot off at a dead gallop, scattering the chickens that pecked at the end of the yard.

Juan watched her go. Perhaps he ought to accept Rose's offer of work, he thought, and the other offers she'd been making to him with her long, fluttering eyelashes. Wouldn't Charlotte be surprised?

But no, the more he thought of striking back at Charlotte, the less he wanted to. Spoiled and temperamental Charlotte might be, but there was, hidden within her, a sweetness that was completely missing in Rose Fontaine, a sweetness that he longed to experience again. In spite of everything, he found himself yearning to see Charlotte, yearning to make things right with her. It was silly to pretend that they were finished with each other. There was something between them, a fire that would never be put out.

Soon Juan found himself saddling his horse. It was late afternoon, almost dusk, and a storm was forming overhead. But a storm was not enough to stop him. Not when he was determined to see Charlotte.

Chapter Six

Charlotte looked at the big cans of paint, their round tops as shiny as silver coins. They'd just arrived that afternoon, and now that the workday was over and she was alone at the stable site, she felt her heart racing with excitement.

Work on the buildings had gone fast. The weeks of winter had slipped away and now it was almost March. Even so, everything wasn't quite done. The painting wouldn't start until next week. Charlotte couldn't wait: She was dying to know what the stables would look like with the new paint on them. *I'll just open one of the cans and look at it*, she thought. *There isn't any harm in that*.

But once the can of creamy white paint was opened, she had to open one of the cans of green as well. And once that was done, she found herself longing to see how the two would look together. The only thing to do about *that*, of course, was to find a couple of brushes and begin to paint.

Just this one little square, Charlotte told herself. *It won't take long. I'll be done in no time*.

Earlier that day her father had spoken to her about the amount of time she spent at the site and about the number of times she arrived at the dinner table just in time for dessert.

"You said you wanted me to take this seriously," she had protested, "and that's what I'm doing."

"But not so seriously that you forget your family," George Harmon replied. "It's as if you've given up everything else in life. Why, you haven't been to a party in weeks!"

Charlotte smiled mischievously. "I didn't know parties were so important to you."

"They aren't. But they used to be important to you. Very important."

"Maybe I've changed," Charlotte replied. She could see that her father was truly concerned about her. "Don't worry about me, Papa. I'm fine. Really."

George Harmon leaned back in his big chair. "There's a new family in the area," he began. "I don't think you've had time to meet them yet. Their name is Fontaine. Three brothers and a sister. I met the oldest brother in San Antonio a few days ago. They're having a big party next week, and, of course, we're invited. I'd like you to come."

"But, Papa—" Charlotte started to protest. She had heard rumors about the Fontaine clan, about their amazing wealth and the magnificent house they'd had built for them. Belle Monde, it was said, was a nearly exact replica of the Louisiana plantation the family had owned before the Civil War.

"The sister, Rose, is just your age," George Harmon continued, hoping to entice her. "You might become friends with her."

Charlotte wrinkled her nose. "Oh, Papa, she's probably spoiled and selfish and not interested in anything but herself and her clothes and her beaus."

Suddenly both father and daughter began to laugh. They began to laugh because, without meaning to, Charlotte had described herself as she'd been just a few months ago.

"I'll think about going to the party," she promised her father at last. "Truly. And I'll try not to miss any more dinners."

Now here she was, only a few hours later, still at the stable site while dinner was being served. But as she dipped her brush into the fresh, smooth paint, she felt not a single pang of guilt. Her father would forgive her. He always did. He would even forgive her when she told him she had no intention of going to the Fontaines' party.

She lifted the brush and slapped it against the fresh wood. Drops of white paint, like heavy cream, splattered all over her, over her face and her arms and her cherry-colored dress. Charlotte painted with dash and vigor. By the time she had a square of the stable wall painted, she had smudges of paint, white and green, all over her.

"You look like the Mexican flag," said a voice behind her, "red, white, and green!"

Charlotte whirled around, her body responding to the voice before she consciously realized who it was. "Juan!"

Instinctively she smiled, smiled because he looked so handsome and because it was so good to see him again. Then, remembering where things stood between them, she forced the smile away.

"The stables are almost done, I see," he said, swinging down from his horse.

"No thanks to you," she retorted.

"It was you who fired me, Charlotte. I did not quit."

"You forced me to fire you," Charlotte said. It wasn't true, she knew it wasn't true, but it was the only thing she could think of to say.

Juan smiled faintly. "Is that what happened? My memory must be faulty. Thank you for correcting me."

"Not at all." Turning away, Charlotte dipped a brush into the green paint can. She was experimenting with the trim, and green paint, as dark and shiny as pine needles, dripped from the end of the brush.

"I think you've missed me, Charlotte."

Startled by his nearness, she jumped. Juan was handsome, so handsome that he made her heart feel like butter sizzling in a skillet. *But I can't control him!* she thought. *How can I want to be with someone I have no control over?* "Go home," she said, afraid of letting her thoughts show on her face.

"Yes," Juan said, "you really *have* missed me."

He was stepping toward her, so broad-shouldered and graceful it seemed as if he were floating. But no, Charlotte realized, the dizzy, floating feeling was hers. It started in her knees and spread right up to her head.

"Stay back, Juan. Stay back or—"

"Or what?"

Suddenly the hand holding the paintbrush shot out. A wide, green splash of green appeared on Juan's shirt front.

Faster than lightning he swooped down, grabbed the brush she'd left in the white paint, and painted a white stripe across her skirt.

Charlotte was aghast. "How dare you!" she cried. "How dare you!" Dipping her brush into the green paint again, she lunged at him.

They painted each other from head to toe, trading slaps of the brush until they were both exhausted. It was Juan who began to laugh first. After so many days of worry about rustlers and so many nights of dreaming about Charlotte, the laughter felt good.

"You're horrible," Charlotte said indignantly. "Look what you've done to me! Just look! And you think it's funny! I'm going to tell my father. He'll have you thrown off Cielo Hermoso at once."

Juan caught her arm. "You're not going to do anything of the sort," he told her. He was still laughing. "Admit it, Charlotte. This is the most fun you've had since you fired me, isn't it?"

Against her will she started to grin. She couldn't help herself. "Yes." The sight of him, of handsome, dignified Juan Ortiz covered with blobs and splatters of paint, struck her as hysterically funny. She laughed until her lungs ached.

"Does this mean," he asked at last, "that you wish to hire me back?"

"I didn't say that," she replied, her laughter subsiding.

"Good. Because I'm not sure I'd come back."

His words caught her by surprise. "What do you mean?" Juan had found a scrap of rag. Dampening it with turpentine from a can, he began, carefully, to wipe the paint from her face.

Charlotte didn't protest, but let him do it. "I asked you what you meant," she repeated.

"I mean that you are too difficult to work with."

He wiped a splatter of paint from her nose. Charlotte felt a little tingle of excitement. "I don't know why you think so," she said.

"If I came back to work with you," Juan said, wiping away still another drop of paint and sending still another shiver down her spine, "our arrangement would have to be different. We would have to be truly partners. None of this loco firing."

"Who says I even want you back?" Charlotte asked.

Juan did not answer. Instead he settled his arms firmly around her waist, drew her to him, and kissed her.

Charlotte felt as if the whole world were exploding. "Yes, I want you to come back, Juan," she said between his kisses. "Nothing's the same without you. I'll never fire you again. I promise."

He looked down at her, his dark eyes full of amusement. "I must have it in writing," he said.

"Yes," she said. "Yes, anything. Juan?"

"What?"

"Will you kiss me again?"

For the next few days Charlotte lived in paradise. Only it was better than paradise, she told herself, because in paradise spirits floated without bodies. Here on earth, on Cielo Hermoso, things had shape and form. She had only to go to the building site to see Juan's tall, lean form striding between the almost-finished stables. She had only to catch his eye to see his wonderful, heartwarming smile.

With Juan back the crew became efficient once again. Before Charlotte knew it, the painting began.

One afternoon she looked out and saw her friend Maggie McNeill riding up to the back kitchen porch. "I hear your stables are almost finished," Maggie said. "Cleve rode over to see Buck last night and told us all about them, so I thought I'd come take a look."

Charlotte smiled. "As soon as I finish lunch for the crew, Maggie," she said, "I'll give you a guided tour. You will eat with us, won't you?"

Maggie nodded, studying her old friend. There was a glow to Charlotte that Maggie recognized almost at once, a glow that didn't have anything to do with finished stables or the horse business.

"How is Juan?" Maggie asked at last, her voice deliberately casual.

"Wonderful," Charlotte replied and, seeing Maggie's inquisitive glance, told her everything that had happened in the last few days. "Juan can be so stubborn, Maggie," Charlotte finished, her green eyes shining like polished jade, "but I still have all these wonderful feelings whenever I'm near him . . . whenever I even think about him. I've never felt this way about anyone before. Never."

Maggie smiled, understanding the softness that had come into Charlotte's voice as she talked about Juan. "I'm happy for you, Charlotte," she said, her eyes sparkling. "I always believed you and Juan belonged together. I can't tell you how upset I was when I rode by La Jota and saw Rose Fontaine's horse tethered outside."

Charlotte's eyes flashed and Maggie instantly realized her mistake. Charlotte obviously didn't know anything about Rose's visits to Juan!

"What about Rose Fontaine?" Charlotte demanded, her voice full of cactus thorns. "How many times did you see her horse there?"

"Twice," Maggie said reluctantly. "But I'm sure it wasn't important. I'm sure it was just Rose trying to stir something up. I hear she's a terrible flirt, and—"

Charlotte interrupted her. "When did you see Rose's horse, Maggie?"

"Days ago. I can't remember. It isn't really important, is it, Charlotte? You're the one Juan cares about."

"Maggie, please! I have to know."

So Maggie searched her memory until she came up with the dates. The first time Rose had visited Juan had been the day he failed to show up for work at Cielo Hermoso. (*The day he told me he had personal business!* Charlotte thought with a shock.) The second time had been a week ago, the same day he'd ridden over to Cielo Hermoso.

Right out of Rose's arms and into mine! How could he? How could he? Charlotte felt hurt and angry and betrayed. She didn't for a minute believe Maggie when she said that the visits had probably been innocent. She understood girls like Rose Fontaine too well for that.

"What are you going to do?" Maggie asked.

Charlotte considered. She wanted to march right down to the site and have it out with Juan. She wanted to cry and scream and pour out her hurt feelings. But no, that was the mistake she'd made before. She'd been far too open with Juan as it was. He knew everything she was thinking and feeling, knew how fiercely she desired his kisses. She'd done something with Juan that she'd never done with any boy before: She'd let him see her as she really was. She'd let him see inside of her, all her feelings and her hopes, all her wishes and her fears. Most of all, she'd let him see how much she cared for him. *Well*, she thought, setting her chin, *that's a mistake I won't make this time!*

I don't know what I'm going to do exactly," she told Maggie. Suddenly she remembered the Fontaine party, the ball that was to be held tomorrow night. "I have an idea, though."

By the time Maggie left a few hours later, Charlotte's feelings had simmered down a little. *Maybe Maggie is right after all*, she told herself. *Maybe there is some explanation.*

Her heart lifted a little at the thought. She wanted to believe it. Goodness, how she wanted to believe it!

She waited until the crew had left for the day, waited until she and Juan were alone. She had her plan firmly in mind, and nothing, not even the rush of emotion she felt as he stepped forward to kiss her, was going to turn her aside.

"I was thinking," she said smoothly, nestling in his arms, "that it's time for you to get to know my father better. He doesn't know how we feel about each other yet, but I think he will approve, once he gets to know you."

"And if he doesn't approve?" Juan asked teasingly.

"He will. I'm certain of it. Will you come to dinner at the house, Juan?"

His lips grazed her forehead. "Of course. A delightful idea, senorita *mia*."

"Good. Tomorrow night, then?"

Juan remembered Rose Fontaine, remembered that he had to go to her ball and turn down the work she'd offered him. He could send a message, of course, or even ride to Belle Monde himself to tell her, but that wasn't how he wanted to handle the matter. He distrusted Rose and knew that she would not easily take no for an answer. If he sent a note, she would ride to La Jota to try to make him change his mind. If he rode to Belle Monde in person, she would try to make him stay. No. At the ball, surrounded by many other people, was the way to turn down her request. "I cannot tomorrow," he replied.

She pulled away from him. "Why not?"

He considered telling her the truth. Under any other circumstances he would have. But things had been going so well between them lately, he didn't want to spoil things. If she knew he was going to Rose Fontaine's party, she might get the wrong idea. She might think he wanted to flirt and dance with other girls.

After weighing all the possibilities, Juan decided to remain silent. Charlotte wasn't going to the ball herself, he was certain of that. She hadn't been to a single party since work on the stables had begun. She would find out later that he'd been there, of course, but by then he would have found a way to explain things to her.

"I have some personal business to attend to tomorrow," he said.

"Can't it wait?"

"No, it can't."

Anger flashed in Charlotte's mind. She remembered the last time personal business had kept Juan away from Cielo Hermoso. That had been the first time Rose Fontaine's horse had appeared outside La Jota. So her suspicions were right! Juan, who was at this very moment holding her so tenderly, was flirting with Rose Fontaine behind her back! With a sharp frown Charlotte jerked away from him. She almost enjoyed the look of puzzled surprised that washed across his face.

"*Querida*—," he began.

"Oh, *querida* yourself!" she snapped. "Go attend to your personal business! See if I care!"

Turning sharply, she walked swiftly away from him. If Juan thought he was going to make a fool of her, he was in for a surprise. She hadn't had the least desire to go to Rose Fontaine's ball before, but she was going now!

Chapter Seven

Rose Fontaine looked over the second-floor railing that circled the gallery. Below her, in Belle Monde's huge ballroom, couples swirled to lively tunes.

"Happy, Rosebud?"

At the sound of her childhood nickname, Rose turned to face her oldest brother. Twelve years older than she was, Darcy seemed more like a father than a brother to her. Rose gave him a jubilant smile.

"Oh, Darcy, I didn't think this would ever happen. Ever! I'm going to be happy here at Belle Monde, I can just tell!"

At that moment Darcy's wife appeared. "I told you, Rose," Rebecca said, "that if you're going to wear that low-cut gown, you have to keep your shawl with you. Where is it?"

"It's around somewhere," Rose answered, frowning. She didn't like the spiritless, modest woman who was her sister-in-law.

"Oh, leave her be, Becca," Darcy urged gently. "It's her first ball, after all. Her first *real* one, anyway."

As her brother and his wife moved off, Rose smiled a smile of deep satisfaction. She could twist her brother around her finger as she did with all men. And the ballroom floor below her was, fortunately, absolutely littered with men, men just waiting to be curled around her fingers.

Rose Fontaine had waited a long time for this moment. She would never forgive the Civil War for coming along just as she was beginning to think about parties and balls, just as she would never forgive the Yankee soldiers who had destroyed her family's Louisiana plantation. But now, in Texas, they were starting all over again. Looking down at the dancing couples, Rose felt as if it had all been created for her alone. She would rule it like a princess, and soon everyone would forget that Charlotte Harmon even existed.

Charlotte Harmon. It was a name she had heard entirely too often since coming to Texas. Everyone told her how beautiful Charlotte was, everyone told her how popular Charlotte was; everyone told her how wonderful it would be if she and Charlotte could become friends.

Not likely, Rose thought, lifting her nose in the air. *I only hope what they say is true, that Charlotte Harmon doesn't go to parties anymore.*

"What are you doing up here, Rosebud?" It was her brother Etienne. Offering her his arm, he added, "Let me take you down."

Rose shook her head quickly. "Oh, no, I want to go down alone. You *can* do me a favor, though."

"Anything, Sis. Just name it."

"Go ask the musicians to play something dramatic."

"Sure enough."

A minute later the lively dance music switched to the deep, moving strains of "My Old Kentucky Home." Rose waited until the dancers glided to a halt. Then, lifting her creamy white skirt in her fingertips to reveal teasing glimpses of frothy petticoats, conscious of the cascade of silk roses that clustered at the waist of her gown, Rose started down the stairs. A murmur of approval rippled through the crowd, and Rose felt the eyes of every man in the room turn to her. It was all just as she'd planned. So much for Charlotte Harmon, she thought. By the end of tonight no one would even remember who Charlotte Harmon was.

"Kentucky Home" ended and the musicians swung into a reel. Rose, now at the bottom of the stairs, chose a partner from the dozen young men who'd flocked to greet her. As she glided around the ballroom, switching from one partner to another, she felt the scalding eyes of angry young women on her. *As if I cared!* she thought contemptuously. *If they can't hold onto their beaus, it's hardly my fault.*

Rose wasn't sure how long she had danced before she stopped to rest. If it hadn't been for the tightness of her stays, she was certain she could have gone on dancing forever. But her maid, Renée, had laced her so tightly, she felt faint. She was standing near the refreshment table trying to catch her breath, surrounded by a crowd of admirers, when Juan Ortiz arrived.

Rose's eyes flew to him at once. He looked, she thought, handsome and tall and breathtakingly exciting. In the flurry of the evening, in the pleasure of stealing away other girls' beaus, she'd forgotten about inviting him. But now her glance cut through the crowd, and making a way for herself, she walked directly up to him.

"Why, Juan," she said breathlessly, "I'm so glad you could come. I didn't think I'd have anyone to dance with!" And before he had time to reply, she pulled him onto the dance floor with her.

Even though Charlotte was nowhere in sight, Juan felt ill at ease. The way Rose was looking at him and the pressure of her hand in his made him feel as if he were doing something wrong. As Rose coaxed him into a second dance, he cleared his throat uncomfortably.

"I came to give you your answer, senorita," Juan said.

"Answer to what?" Rose asked languidly.

"About the building you wanted me to work on." Juan had made up his mind once and for all just a few hours ago. Another calf was missing from La Jota. Perhaps it had just strayed, but Juan didn't think so. La Jota, vulnerable to rustlers as it was, needed him. Until they were taken care of, he was not free to make choices. "I cannot work for your family, Rose," Juan said.

To his amazement Rose only laughed in reply. "Business, business, business. I don't want to hear a single word about business tonight, not when you are such a wonderful dancer!"

"But—"

Rose put her fingers to his lips. "I'm serious! Not a word. We'll discuss it another time."

Juan felt frustrated and not at all certain what to do about Rose. *Now that I am here*, he told himself, *I will make the best of it. I will at least be able to talk to the other ranchers*. But when he tried to get away from Rose, he was unsuccessful. No sooner would he be talking to Randall Morgan or Quinn Farrell or one of the Judd brothers than Rose would glide up to him, insisting that she could find no other partner.

It was during one of these turns around the dance floor that Juan looked up and saw Charlotte standing at the entranceway of the ballroom.

It wasn't just his imagination, he realized. At the sight of Charlotte Harmon everyone in the ballroom, including Rose Fontaine herself, gasped in surprise.

Charlotte had never looked more beautiful. She was wearing her best gown of deep blue velvet, but a gown that was much transformed. Having decided to attend the Fontaine's ball, Charlotte had also decided that she must look spectacular. In a moment of inspiration she'd broken apart her favorite necklace, a long double strand of tiny crystal beads, and stayed up half the night sewing them on the dress. Scattered over the shoulders of the dress and ending in a showery cascade at the hem, the beads glistened and caught the light and gave it back again. Against the deep blue velvet they looked like a shower of stars spread out against the sky. Wrapped in the dress, Charlotte looked like a creature from another planet, someone too beautiful to have come from earth. Even Teyah and Maggie, who stood beside her, paled in comparison. For one single, perfect moment Charlotte Harmon had no equal.

I hate her! Rose thought furiously. For she knew, without anyone having to tell her, that the beautiful creature standing before her was Charlotte Harmon. *I'll never forgive her for this!*

Charlotte, meanwhile, was oblivious to the gasps of approval and stares of admiration she

received. She saw only one thing in the crowded
ballroom: She saw Juan, *her* Juan, in Rose
Fontaine's arms.

For one moment she stood uncertainly,
wanting both to flee and to sail forward and slap
Rose across the face. Then Rose's youngest
brother, handsome, twenty-one-year-old Trenton, appeared before her.

"You will dance with me, won't you, Miss
Harmon?" he asked.

Charlotte glanced again at Juan. Rose Fontaine's hand was planted firmly on his shoulder.
"Why, I'd be delighted to dance with you," she
replied, tipping her head just enough to make the
diamonds in her ears flash. "Delighted!"

Just as soon as he could, Juan made his way
to Charlotte's side. It wasn't easy. First, he had to
disentangle himself from Rose Fontaine. Second,
he had to cut through the throng of young men
who'd gathered around Charlotte.

As he approached her, Juan felt his heart
beating rapidly. She was angry with him, he
knew; but even so, he could not dismiss the joy he
felt. She was beautiful, shining with an inner
fierceness that no other girl possessed. As soon as
things between them were put right, as soon as
he explained why he'd had to come here, he
looked forward to dancing with her. Dancing
with her and later, on the wide terrace that
overlooked the majestic plains, sweeping her into
his arms.

"Charlotte," he began, "I need to talk to
you." He stopped. Charlotte, with eyebrows
raised, was looking at him as if they'd never even
met.

"As you can see," she said, gesturing to the young man at her side, "I'm busy right now."

"Charlotte, please, I know you are angry but—"

"Really, Juan, this is hardly the time." With that, she turned her back on him.

Swiftly Juan seized her elbow and spun her around. "Don't play these silly games, Charlotte. I am going to speak with you!" With a sharp, dismissing nod he pulled her away from her partner.

Charlotte's cheeks flushed with anger. "Just what do you think you're doing?" she questioned. "You act as if you own me."

Juan gave her a long look, remembering the kisses they'd shared. "We own each other, senorita."

It was the wrong thing to say because Charlotte wasn't remembering those kisses at all. She was remembering the fact that Rose Fontaine's horse had been seen not once but twice at La Jota. "That," she said, lifting her elbow and pulling it away from him, "is where you're wrong. As for us needing to talk, I can't think of a single thing you could say that I'd care to listen to."

"Now just a minute, Charlotte, you've got the wrong idea—I was just—"

Before he could go on, Trenton Fontaine came up to them. "They're playing the Virginia Reel again, Charlotte," he said with a smile. "They're playing it just for us. If," he added with a swift glance at Juan, "you're finished here, that is."

Charlotte turned to him, crystal beads sparkling. "I'm finished, Trenton," she said with a

sweet smile. And giving him her hand, sailed off
without so much as a backward glance.

Flirting, Charlotte thought, *is something you
just don't forget. It's like walking or like breathing.* She
hadn't flirted in months, she hadn't wanted to,
but that didn't mean she'd forgotten how. Taking
stock of the ballroom, she caught the eyes of at
least a dozen young men. With a glance at once
haughty and inviting, she managed to convey to
them the message that they might, just might, if
they were lucky, be allowed to dance with her. It
was no accident that the young men she encour-
aged most were those most closely connected to
Rose Fontaine: her brother Trenton and her
favorite beaus. Because it wasn't just Juan
Charlotte wanted to get back at, it was also Rose.
If it weren't for Rose, none of this would be
happening. If it weren't for Rose . . .

Charlotte consoled herself with the fact that
Rose Fontaine's evening had ended the moment
she arrived. A sixth sense and Rose's own furious
glances told her it was true. She was upstaging
Rose with every dance, outshining the girl who
was supposed to be the star of the evening. Two
years ago that fact alone would have made
Charlotte deliriously happy. But two years ago
there had been no Juan Ortiz. Now no amount of
admiration, of invitations to dance, could make
up for the fact that she had arrived to find Juan in
the arms of someone else.

Juan, like Charlotte, was miserable. And
confused. Always before, he'd enjoyed
Charlotte's displays of spirit, her frequent out-
bursts of fiery temper. But this outburst he hadn't
enjoyed at all. Why was she so angry with him?
Why was she so unwilling to let him explain the

situation? And why, above all, was she dancing with everyone, *everyone*, except him?

"If someone tried to break my heart," said a voice in Juan's ear, "I'd rather die than let her see it."

Juan looked at Rose, understanding at once what she meant. "You are right," he said, his mouth settling into a firm, handsome line. "Absolutely right." And extending his hand to her, he led her out onto the dance floor.

Charlotte saw Juan and Rose and felt a pang of alarm. For the last half hour, ever since she'd walked away from him, Juan had followed her around the room with sad, wounded eyes. She'd expected him to behave in exactly the same way for the rest of the evening. She'd even expected him to approach her again. But she had never for an instant expected him to take the floor with Rose Fontaine. The fact that he did indicated to Charlotte that it was Rose he cared for after all.

Charlotte, dancing in the arms of Evan Judd, was stunned. She'd meant to make Juan miserable, had meant to teach him a lesson. But she had always intended, when he had suffered enough, to take him back.

The sight of Juan and Rose dancing together made Charlotte miserable. The moment the ball ended, the moment she was seated in her father's large carriage with Teyah on one side of her and Maggie McNeill on the other, she burst into tears.

"What's wrong?" asked Cleve. He was seated in the backseat with Buck Crawford.

"Shh," Teyah answered over her shoulder. "Leave her alone."

"Man trouble," Buck whispered, and Maggie's warning, annoyed glance told him he was right.

George and Lavinia Harmon, on the high front springboard seat of the carriage, didn't hear the low sobs behind them.

"I hate him," Charlotte choked, wiping tears away with her fingers. "I wish I'd never met him. I wish a steer would trample him to death so I'd never have to see him again!"

Above her head Teyah's topaz-colored eyes met Maggie's blue ones in a glance of understanding. Both girls knew exactly how Charlotte felt, and both knew that, eventually, the storm of tears would pass.

"You don't really feel that way, Charlotte," Teyah said.

"I do," Charlotte insisted, tears springing to her eyes again. "I do hate him! I do!"

Maggie laid a comforting hand on Charlotte's shoulder. "Now, that's a fine thing to say about someone who loves you as much as Juan does."

Charlotte's head jerked up. "*Love* me? How can you possibly say that, Maggie?"

"Just a feeling I have. Besides, I saw the look on Juan's face when you were dancing with Trenton Fontaine."

"As if he cared! He danced with Rose all night!"

"Just to hide his feelings, Charlotte," Maggie said, and added, "he really does care for you."

Charlotte didn't answer. Instead she raised her head and looked at the bright, distant stars. *How lucky they are, not to have any feelings*, she thought. *If I could be anything right now, I'd want to be a star*.

But she didn't really mean it, not any more than she'd meant it when she said she hated Juan.

Chapter Eight

Juan lay awake in the pale dawn. There was an open place between the logs that formed the roof, and through it he could see a single bright star. The star reminded him of the beads on Charlotte's dress and of the diamonds in her ears.

Charlotte. Always before, her name had brought a smile to his lips. This morning it brought a frown, a frown of anger and confusion and, though he hated to admit it, pain. Juan had only to remember the sight of Charlotte dancing with Trenton Fontaine to make the pain frighteningly strong. Why hadn't she given him a chance to talk to her, a chance to explain things? Why had she turned away from him so coolly and spent the rest of the evening in the arms of other young men?

There can be only one reason, Juan thought. *She doesn't care about me. What happened between us was only a flirtation for her, nothing more. If she cared, truly cared, she would not have walked away from me last night!*

At that thought the pain that lay like a heavy rock on his chest reached all the way to his heart. He had been nothing more than a toy to Charlotte; he had been a fool to think otherwise.

His cheeks burned at the thought. There was only one way to restore his crushed pride, and that was to have nothing more to do with her. The new agreement between them, the agreement he had in writing, said neither of them could fire the other. It said nothing whatsoever about neither of them being allowed to quit. And on Monday morning, just as soon as the sun was up, that's what he intended to do.

"Juan?"

His father's voice startled him. He looked toward his father's bed and saw that it was empty. Instead his father, fully dressed, was standing in the doorway. Instantly an alarm went off inside Juan, pushing even his thoughts of Charlotte aside.

"What's wrong, Father?"

Roberto Ortiz strode into the room. His dark-eyed, handsome face was creased with lines of worry. "The rustlers are back."

Juan leaped out of bed, reaching automatically for his clothes, his glance veering toward the gun that hung from pegs on the wall above him. He knew they would come back. Now the moment had arrived.

"I will go after them," Juan said. Dressed now, he reached for his gun.

Roberto Ortiz stopped him. "No," he said, his voice quiet but very powerful. "That is what they will expect this time. I have a different plan."

"What is it?"

"I have set a trap. I moved our best cattle into the western pasture, the one just over the hill from here. You go about your work today as if nothing were wrong, as if we suspected nothing. But your gun must be loaded, Juan, and your

horse, hidden in the stable, saddled and ready."
He paused and looked into his son's face. "You
are not afraid of facing them, are you?"

"Of course not," Juan replied.

"*Bueno.* I will ride out as if I, also, suspect
nothing. But I will be ready on the other side of
the pasture, hidden and watching. The rustlers
will not be able to resist those fat, healthy cattle,
and they will try to get them. When they do, I will
fire a shot. You will ride from one side, I from the
other. We will catch the rustlers between us."

Juan considered. "How many are there?"

"Six. I picked up their tracks several miles
away. They are still searching the other pastures
for cattle, but they will find their way here
eventually."

"It's dangerous," Juan said. "Six against two,
and they will be armed."

"Yes," Roberto Ortiz said, "but it is our
chance to stop them once and for all, to catch
them and turn them over to the authorities in San
Antonio. Are you willing?"

Juan nodded. There was nothing he wanted
more than to put the thieves behind bars, where
they belonged. "Of course."

"I will go, then," Roberto Ortiz said. "You
are to saddle your horse, ready your guns, then
act as if you suspect nothing. When you hear my
gunshot, come as fast as you can. *Comprendo?*"

"Yes," Juan answered, "I understand completely. Good luck, Father."

"And you, Juan."

Love. Charlotte had tossed and turned all
night over the word. Could it be that Maggie was
right? Could it be that Juan really did love her?

By dawn Charlotte had decided that there was only one thing to do: She would ride to Juan's and find out how he really *did* feel about her.

As she dressed, she imagined Juan confessing his feelings to her. Maybe he would beg her to forgive him for dancing with Rose last night. Well, wouldn't that be something? Charlotte smiled because she liked this idea. Wouldn't it be wonderful to see Juan begging for her forgiveness? It would serve him right, too, if she didn't give it to him. It would serve him right if instead of accepting his apology, she got back on her horse and galloped away.

Except that she wasn't at all sure she could do that. Juan was irresistible to her, and her own feelings were as mysterious to her as Juan's were. Whenever she thought of him, whenever she remembered the times he had kissed her or the times they hadn't been fighting, a sweet feeling flooded her thoughts like sunshine.

Oh, Juan, she thought as she guided her horse toward La Jota, *why do you make me feel this way? It's never been like this with any other boy. Not Billy Joe Briscoe or Trenton Fontaine or anyone. When I'm with you I feel so . . . so different. Why?*

A sudden thought pushed its way into Charlotte's thoughts. Love. If Juan loved her, then maybe she loved him too. But no, she told herself swiftly. That couldn't be. Could it?

Juan was sorting nails in La Jota's yard when he heard hoofbeats. With an effort of will he forced himself not to look up, not to acknowledge the pang of fear that cramped his stomach. What if the plan had gone wrong? What if the rustlers were riding toward him even now?

There is only one horse, he assured himself, listening carefully. *I hear only one horse*. He scooped up another handful of nails. The straight, usable ones in one bucket, the bent ones in another bucket to be straightened later.

The hoofbeats slowed to a walk. "Juan?"

He looked up abruptly. Charlotte! She was the last person he'd expected to see, the very last. Before he could recover from his shock, she was off her horse and walking toward him.

"Hello, Juan."

At her words the pain he'd felt in the minutes before dawn came racing back to him. How could she be standing here, looking as glorious as a Texas wildflower, looking at him as if she'd done nothing at all to hurt him? "What are you doing here, Charlotte?" he asked abruptly.

It wasn't what she'd expected, not at all. Juan didn't look the least apologetic. Worse than that, he didn't look the least in love. Instead it was as if he were wearing a mask, a mask that hid his feelings from her. Reflexively her chin jerked up proudly. "I thought it might be a good idea for us to talk," she said, her voice showing no trace of her tangled emotions.

"Talk about what?" Juan asked.

"About last night." She waited for his face to change, for him to give some signal that he really did care for her, as Maggie said he did, but he didn't.

"What about last night?" It was difficult for Juan to hide his feelings, difficult for him not to show Charlotte his hurt, but he was determined not to. It would only make things worse.

Charlotte, standing in the yard of La Jota, began to feel extremely foolish. Maggie had been wrong. Juan didn't love her. He didn't even care for her enough to stop sorting nails. This is terrible, she thought, terrible.

"What about last night?" Juan asked again.

Charlotte cleared her throat. "Well . . . well, I just wanted to say that I hope nothing happened to make you feel, er, uncomfortable. I mean, things like that are going to happen. We're going to run into each other sometimes, at parties or in town. I don't want there to be any hard feelings."

Juan stared at her, unable to believe his ears. *I don't want there to be any hard feelings.* As if it had all been a game! Yet he could not bring himself to hate her. Standing in his yard, her wide green eyes catching flecks of gold from the sun, her riding crop tapping decisively against the toe of one boot, she was still the most exciting girl he had ever met. Nothing would ever change that.

Suddenly a menacing thought came to him. The rustlers! Charlotte was in danger. He must, *must*, get her off La Jota. "Of course there are no hard feelings," he said brusquely. "Is that all you came to say, senorita?"

"Yes."

"Then you will kindly be on your way," Juan replied. "As you see, I am very busy."

"But—"

Juan stepped toward her and, seizing her elbow, propelled her toward her horse. "I am very busy!" he said again in a harsh tone Charlotte had never heard him use before. "If you wish to waste time, that is your business, but do it with someone else. I have work to do!"

Biting her lip, stunned by Juan's harshness, Charlotte mounted her horse and rode away swiftly, eager to put La Jota behind her as quickly as possible. Juan didn't love her, he never would, and coming to La Jota had been a terrible mistake.

Stinging tears streaked down her face, and she swiped at them angrily, trying to clear her vision. If she didn't pay attention to where she was going, she would get lost. Blinking, she reined her horse to a halt and looked toward the horizon. There, prancing along its sunny rim, was a golden blond horse. And riding on that horse, headed directly toward La Jota, was Rose Fontaine!

Charlotte's heart jerked in her chest. Rose! So that's why Juan had been so brusque, so eager to get rid of her—because he was expecting Rose any minute.

For a moment Charlotte simply sat, staring at the distant figure on the horse. Now a new pain flooded through her, a pain so deep and biting that, for a moment, she thought it would kill her. Maybe Juan didn't love her, but she loved him. She knew that now. There was no denying it. Only real love could send such pain racing through her.

Rose Fontaine cantered across the gently rolling prairie, so focused on her own thoughts that she never even noticed Charlotte's horse in the distance. *Today I put my plan into action*, she thought, smiling to herself.

Rose was a girl who didn't believe in letting any grass grow under her feet. Juan Ortiz had left her party in a bad mood, hurt and angry over Charlotte's behavior toward him. Today, Rose thought, some of those feelings might have softened. Juan might even be foolish enough to think that he liked Charlotte again. Rose didn't intend to let that happen. She intended to ride to Juan and remind him, in very subtle ways, how terrible Charlotte had been. She was even prepared to tell him, though it wasn't true, that Charlotte had agreed to go riding with her brother Trenton that afternoon.

Rose's smile widened. Once Juan was reminded of all this, he would drop into her hands like a ripe apple. And oh, how hurt and humbled Charlotte Harmon would be by it all!

Shots, as rapid as Fourth of July fireworks, rang out in Rose's ears. They'd come from the direction of La Jota, no doubt about it. Drawing her horse to a halt, she sat for several seconds, her heart beating rapidly. Gunshots always meant trouble. It crossed her mind that Juan might be hurt, might be torn and bleeding. Should she go to him?

Rose sat a moment longer. If she rode forward, she would be putting herself in danger. There was no telling who'd fired the shots or why. Whoever had fired them might just as easily fire at her.

With a swift movement Rose Fontaine wheeled her horse around and headed back to Belle Monde. She would tell her brothers what had happened. They would send help. That was the best thing to do, Rose told herself, and the safest.

As soon as she reached Cielo Hermoso, Charlotte ran up the stairs to her room and threw herself on the bed. In reply to Lavinia Harmon's inquiries and anxious knocks on her door she said only, "I'm sick, please leave me alone and I'm sure I'll be all right. No, thank you, I'm not hungry. No, please don't send a tray up to my room."

Charlotte cried until her face was red and swollen, cried until she began to feel as sick as she'd told Lavinia she was. In the still, hot hours of the afternoon she lay on her bed, staring at the ceiling, and thought, over and over to herself, *Everything's over. My life is over. Oh, I hate him, hate him so much!*

She'd been sleeping, exhausted by her tears, when a fresh knock came at the door, a knock that didn't sound at all like Lavinia's. "Who is it?" she asked cautiously.

"Teyah. I want to come in." Without waiting for an answer, Charlotte's half sister pushed open the door. "Oh, Charlotte," she said, tears of sympathy forming in her own eyes when she saw Charlotte's face, "I wish I could make things better!"

Charlotte was touched. "You can't," she said. "No one can." It was hard not to feel a pang of envy. Teyah was so lucky. Teyah had someone to love her; Teyah had Cleve. Suddenly, fresh tears brimmed in Charlotte's eyes. "Oh, Teyah, life is so awful! What's wrong with me? Why can't he love me just a little?" There was no need to explain who the *he* was.

Teyah reached out and took Charlotte's hand. "Maybe he does, Charlotte."

"And act the way he acted last night?"

"Well, maybe he loves you and doesn't know it. That's how it was with me. I loved Cleve a long time before I knew it. Maybe that's how it will be with you and Juan."

Charlotte shook her head. "No," she whispered. "How it happened for you, how it happened for Maggie—it will never happen that way for me. There's something wrong with me, Teyah. I know that now. There's something so wrong with me that nobody will ever, ever love me!"

Teyah reached out and touched her half sister's shoulder. "Everybody feels that way, Charlotte. I know I did. Remember last year, when I thought I loved Juan and ran away because he didn't feel the same way about me? I thought everything would be fine if I could just get back to the Comanche and to a boy I'd known there. I wanted someone to love me so much, and I was afraid that it would never, ever happen."

Charlotte didn't look up, but her sobs quieted as Teyah continued: "Then Cleve came after me, riding alone into Comanche country to find me, and I realized that he'd loved me all along. I'd been so busy *looking* for love that I didn't see it when it was staring right at me. That's the way love is, Charlotte. When you stop looking for it, you see that it's been looking for you all along."

Charlotte didn't answer. Her thoughts were too confused, too tangled and painful. Somehow, though, Teyah's words helped. After a while she reached out and squeezed Teyah's hand. Without hesitation Teyah squeezed Charlotte's hand in reply. No words were said. No words were needed. Both girls felt, at last, that they were truly sisters.

Teyah was still sitting with Charlotte when a sudden commotion was heard downstairs.

"What is it?" Charlotte asked.

Teyah went to the door, opened it, and stood listening. In a moment Charlotte came and stood behind her. There were voices, voices she didn't recognize, talking to her father. Fragments of what they said floated up to her.

"The Ortiz place . . . rustlers . . . Ortiz shot . . . no, not the father, the son . . . lost a lot of blood, might not live . . . ."

Suddenly Charlotte was flying down the stairs. "I want my horse saddled," she cried.

Her father, Cleve, and Lavinia, clustered at the bottom of the stairs with the oldest Fontaine brother, looked up at her with startled eyes.

"This is nothing for you to get mixed up in, Charlotte," her father said sternly. "We'll take care of the rustlers. I'm going to ride to San Antonio and talk to the Texas Rangers about it now."

"Rustlers?!" Charlotte looked at her father in shock. "I don't care about rustlers! They can take every cow in Texas for all I care! It's Juan. If he's hurt, I'm going to go to him! No one's going to stop me!"

Seeing the determined look in her eye, no one tried.

Chapter Nine

*J*uan was unconscious. He'd been unconscious since Charlotte arrived at La Jota, nearly two days ago.

"Please," Charlotte whispered, "please, Juan, you've got to live." She knew he couldn't hear her, but she kept talking to him anyway, murmuring his name over and over again.

"Did you call me, senorita?" asked Luz, her maid, looking up from her embroidery.

"No, Luz," Charlotte answered, her eyes never leaving Juan's face. "No."

Coming to La Jota to take care of Juan had been Charlotte's idea. Luz was along only as a chaperon, only because George Harmon had insisted on it. He hadn't, at first, wanted Charlotte at La Jota at all.

"His father will look after him," George Harmon had said.

"But he needs *me*," Charlotte had cried. "He might not live, don't you understand? He needs me!"

And so, finally, George Harmon had agreed to let Charlotte and Luz go to La Jota. Then he had ridden off to talk to the Texas Rangers in San Antonio because, at last, Roberto Ortiz had decided to turn his problem over to the authorities.

Which he should have done in the first place, Charlotte thought, and added aloud, "Oh, Juan, why didn't you tell anyone? Why were you too proud to ask for help? If you had . . ."

Her thoughts were intruded on by the sound of Luz's needle as it punched through the cloth in her embroidery hoop. Charlotte sighed. If only she could send Luz home, back to Cielo Hermoso. Then she and Juan could be completely alone. But there was no way to send Luz back, not unless she wanted to go back herself.

Charlotte laid her hand against Juan's forehead. It was hot and dry, a bad sign. Blood poisoning, the doctor had told her, was always a danger. Charlotte dipped a rag into a basin of water, squeezed it out, and laid it on Juan's forehead. Then, moving carefully, she began to change the dressing that covered the left side of Juan's chest.

She bit her lip at the sight of the wound, not because she was squeamish but because, every time she looked at the ragged bullet hole, she could not help thinking to herself, How can he live? How can anyone be hurt like this and still live?

Juan had a good chance, the doctor had told her. He'd been able to remove the bullet without too much trouble, and he didn't think the lung had been hit. Juan was a strong young man and, clearly, he had a desire to live. It would depend now on whether internal damage had been done, on whether infection set in, on whether luck was with them.

"Please . . ." Charlotte whispered again.

She was bone-tired because she had not slept in two days. She would not sleep until she knew whether Juan was going to live or not. And so she continued to sit by him, staring down at his silent, handsome face as if it contained the answers to all the questions in her life.

It was midafternoon, two days later, when Charlotte heard hoofbeats in the yard.

"Please see who that is, Luz," she said. There were only two possibilities: The rider would be Juan's father returning from his work in the pastures, or it would be the doctor who came every afternoon to check on Juan's progress.

When Charlotte heard a woman's voice in the yard, she stood up abruptly. Perhaps it was Teyah. She hadn't realized until this moment how she'd been longing to see her half sister.

"Teyah? Is that you? I hope you brought a clean skirt for me because—" As soon as she saw who the visitor was, Charlotte stopped abruptly. "Rose Fontaine! What are you doing here?"

"Why, I'm here to see Juan, of course," Rose said. Unlike Charlotte, whose skirt was crumpled from sitting in it, Rose might have come directly from the fashion houses of New Orleans. Her riding habit, dark green trimmed with flashes of cranberry red, was the newest style. Her hair, shining as if it had been brushed for hours, was braided into a single long plait that swung saucily between her shoulder blades as she walked toward Charlotte. "I've been so very, so *terribly*, worried about him," she said.

Charlotte had almost forgotten how much she disliked Rose just as she'd almost forgotten the terrible hurt of a few nights ago, when Juan had taken Rose in his arms to dance with her. Now those sharp and painful feelings rose inside her. "Juan's unconscious," she said.

"I want to see him anyway," Rose said.

Charlotte stood in the doorway of the cabin, barring the way. "He needs rest," she said.

Color shot into Rose's cheeks. "Just what do you think you're doing? Juan would want to see me. He'd *want* me to be here." A sudden inspiration seized Rose. "After all, we're engaged!"

Her announcement produced the desired effect. Charlotte sagged against the door frame and Rose, smiling triumphantly, sauntered past her. Once inside the ranch house, she went to Juan's side, knelt, and summoned up two very large, very dramatic tears. Her feelings were divided. She did care about Juan, of course she did, and of course she was worried about him. But that worry didn't blot out the satisfaction she felt at hurting Charlotte.

Stealing a glance over her shoulder, Rose saw that Charlotte was still leaning against the open doorway. Look at that skirt, she thought, such a wrinkled mess! And her hair hasn't been properly combed for days. So much for the belle of the county!

For several seconds Charlotte thought she was going to be ill. Engaged. *Engaged!* Could it possibly be? Could Rose Fontaine *possibly* be telling her the truth? Charlotte remembered the party at Belle Monde, remembered a sight that made her heart throb in pain: Juan, hovering near Rose, his head tipped as he whispered something in her ear. Had that been it? It can't be true! a voice within her screamed. And yet . . .

"I'll be back to see him tomorrow," Rose said imperiously, as if Charlotte were just another servant. She lifted the green veil on her hat, and her eyes, deep brown, met Charlotte's. "I hope you won't do anything to keep me away, because if you do, I'll have to tell Juan about it."

"Juan's unconscious," Charlotte said again.

"When he comes to, I'll tell him. I'm sure you wouldn't want that, would you? No? Good. Then we understand each other. I'll see you tomorrow."

Charlotte burned with anger. Until Juan regained consciousness, until she found out what was really going on, there was nothing she could do. As much as she hated Rose, she would have to put up with her. At least for now.

Juan regained consciousness in fits and starts. The first time his eyes fluttered open, Charlotte's heart leapt in delight. He recognized her! He would live!

"Charlotte?" he asked, a confused look in his eyes.

"Yes," she whispered joyously, "yes, Juan, it's me." But even before the words were out of her mouth, his eyes had fluttered closed again, and he was lost in deep sleep.

The next two times he woke up, it was exactly the same. He asked if it was she and what she was doing at La Jota. He didn't seem to remember, from time to time, what was happening. Charlotte was disappointed, but the doctor told her it was very common.

"Don't expect too much," the doctor had warned her, "and don't push him too hard. We're just lucky that he's going to make it."

Charlotte nodded and bit her lip. It was hard. Patience was hard. Especially when, almost every day, she had to put up with Rose Fontaine's visits.

Rose arrived like a visiting queen, treating Luz and Charlotte as if they were both her personal maids.

"Goodness, it's stuffy in here. You seem to know where everything is. Could you bring me a chair? Juan seems to be waking up, he wants water. No, the water in the pitcher is too warm. Could you get us a fresh pitcher from the well?"

Seizing the pitcher, Charlotte stomped off toward the well. What she wanted to do was fill it full of ice-cold water and dump it over Rose Fontaine's head. But what mattered now was Juan, not Rose. Juan needed quiet and rest if he was to recover. A fight between herself and Rose wouldn't do him any good at all. Even worse, Rose might complain to Roberto Ortiz or even to Charlotte's father, and Charlotte might be sent home. No, difficult as it was, Charlotte had no choice but to curb her impulses where Rose was concerned.

One afternoon, when Luz had gone on an errand and Charlotte and Juan were alone in the cabin, Charlotte fell asleep in the chair beside Juan's bed. She woke suddenly, with a stiff neck, certain that she'd heard his voice in her sleep.

"*Hola*, senorita," Juan said, gazing up at her from the bed. There was a slight smile in his voice.

For a moment Charlotte simply sat looking down at him. Something was different. Something, but she wasn't exactly sure what it was. She shook her head, trying to sweep away the cobwebs of sleep. What was it? What was it that was suddenly so different? Then she knew. The fever glow was gone from Juan's eyes. He was looking at her intently, as if he understood everything that had gone on.

"Juan? Oh, Juan!" She laid her hand against his forehead. It was damp but cool. The last traces of fever were gone. A wide, radiant smile spread across her face.

"Charlotte," he said, his voice serious, "we must talk. There is something . . . something I must tell you."

Suddenly she was afraid. A shiver of dread raced up her spine. It's true, she thought leadenly, studying his face. It's true, he's going to marry Rose Fontaine! The glow went out of the room, draining away, just like the hope in her heart.

"I already know," she said.

Juan looked startled. "You do?" She nodded and he reached for her hand. Charlotte bit her lip. Even though she'd lost him, even though he was going to marry Rose, his touch still filled her with excitement.

The sound of hooves sounded suddenly in the yard. Rose. The girl Juan was going to marry. Charlotte stood up abruptly and hurried out into the yard.

"He's awake," she told Rose. "I'll leave the two of you alone."

Without another word Charlotte turned toward the woodpile. Taking up the hatchet, she began the hard job of splitting kindling. Each swing of the hatchet into the crisp, dry wood made a cracking sound. Charlotte felt as if it were her own heart coming apart, ripping apart at its very center.

The longer she worked, the more feelings came bubbling to the surface. Why was she standing out here, blistering her hands, while Rose was in the cabin with Juan? Why? It wasn't fair, not at all. She loved Juan, loved him more than Rose ever would. She was the one who'd cared for Juan all week, not Rose. Rose hadn't lifted a finger. She hadn't done one single solitary thing.

"I'm going now." It was Rose's voice, coming to her suddenly from across the yard. "Juan says he's hungry, so I think it'd be a good idea if you went in and started dinner."

Charlotte's anger, the anger she'd been suppressing all week, bubbled to the surface. "Just a minute," she said, sinking the hatchet to rest in the chopping block and striding toward Rose. "If Juan's hungry, why don't *you* fix him something to eat? You're the one he's going to marry, after all."

Rose, startled, turned to face Charlotte. "I don't know how to cook," she said haughtily.

Charlotte's green eyes flashed. "Then you'd better learn," she shot back, planting her hands on her hips to keep from reaching out and strangling Rose. "If you're going to marry Juan, you'd better learn how to take care of him because if you don't I'll—"

Rose's lips curled in laughter. "You'll what?" she asked mockingly. "What?" Turning, she

started walking again toward her horse, skirts
and braided pigtail swaying impudently.

Charlotte's eyes focused on the swaying
braid. All of her resentment of Rose, all of her
dislike and envy, bubbled to the surface. Dashing
forward, Charlotte caught up with Rose just in
time to seize the glossy braid hanging down her
back. She gave it a sharp tug, a tug that sent Rose
spinning.

Rose whirled around to face Charlotte, fingernails flying. "Let go of me!" she screamed.

"Not until you hear what I have to say!"
Charlotte answered. She wasn't sure what she
wanted to say that she hadn't said already, but it
didn't matter. Before she could utter another
word, Rose's knee caught her in the stomach and
sent her sprawling to the ground.

The yard, like most ranch yards in Texas,
wasn't carpeted with green grass and flowers as
the yard at Cielo Hermoso was. La Jota's yard was
nothing but dirt puddles churned to thick mud by
horses' hooves. Charlotte landing in one of these
muddy places stomach down and face first.
When she raised her head, all she saw was the
heel of Rose's riding boot marching away from
her.

"Oh, no, you don't," Charlotte cried, fling-
ing one arm forward and grabbing a handful of
green riding habit. "If anyone's going to get their
pretty clothes soiled, it's going to be you."

Yanking with all her might, Charlotte pulled
her rival sharply backward. Caught off-balance,
Rose landed in the mud with a satisfying *plop*.
Charlotte had just time enough to smile before
Rose, screeching, came at her again.

The two girls rolled over and over in the mud, pulling each other down, kicking and flailing. Suddenly the sound of laughter interrupted them. Charlotte, the first to recover from her shock, scrambled to her feet.

"Juan!" At first she thought she was seeing things. She wiped the mud from her eyes and looked again. It couldn't be, but it was. There was Juan, pale and thin, leaning in the doorway.

"You shouldn't be up," she said, her worry and her concern for him returning in an instant. "You'll open your wound. Get back into bed."

"And miss the fun? This is better for me than a whole week of rest!"

He was smiling, laughing, at them; and even though she was embarrassed, Charlotte felt a sweet, sharp pang of thankfulness. It was good to see him smile again.

"What have the two of you been fighting about? It couldn't be me, could it?"

There it was again, the old teasing arrogance. For the first time Charlotte knew, really *knew*, that he was going to be all right.

"Over you?" she sniffed. "Over someone who's half-dead? Don't flatter yourself."

Now Juan shifted his attention to Rose. "You tell me, then," he said. "What have you and Charlotte been fighting about?"

Rose, on her feet by now, looked furiously from Juan to Charlotte. Juan wouldn't be satisfied until he had an answer. Realizing that her lie about their engagement was about to be revealed, Rose seized her horse's reins. The only thing to do was get away quickly, before the humiliating truth came to light. She didn't want to wait around to see the triumphant, happy look in Charlotte Harmon's jade-green eyes! Without answering Juan's question, without even pausing to wipe the mud from her face, she mounted the palomino and rode off.

It took Charlotte a full minute to realize what had happened. When she did, a smile came to her lips. Rose had gone! She had fled the scene, leaving Charlotte alone with Juan. Then, suddenly, her senses came back to her. Juan, so recently hovering between life and death, was still leaning in the doorway. Picking up her muddy skirts, she ran to his side.

"You shouldn't be up, didn't you hear me say that? Get back in bed." She reached out her arms and felt his body sag against her as she helped him toward the bed. "Fine girl you picked out to marry," she added under her breath.

Juan heard her. "What did you say? What did you say about the girl I picked to marry?"

Charlotte felt a pain twisting her heart but ignored it. At least she could have her say about Rose. At least she could have that. "I don't think she's right for you, Juan."

"Who?"

"Who? *Who?!* If you weren't still sick, I'd let you fall right here. Rose, that's who."

"Of course Rose isn't right for me," he said.

At first the words, spoken so softly, swept right by Charlotte. Then, suddenly, a flooding warmth filled her. "Not right for you?" she echoed, stopping to look at him. "What do you mean, not right for you? You're going to marry her, aren't you?"

Juan's dark eyes filled with sudden glints of amusement. "You're joking, *querida*. Wherever did you get such an idea?"

"From Rose," Charlotte replied. "Rose told me . . . you mean it isn't true?"

"Of course not," Juan answered.

Charlotte tossed her head. Her cheeks flushed in anger. "Just *wait* until I catch up with her. I'll do more than just pull her braid. She won't have a hair left on her head when I'm through with her!"

Charlotte started toward the door, but Juan caught her hand and held her back. "Rose can wait, *querida*." The lilt was gone from his voice now, and his hand held hers. "I have something to tell you, Charlotte. Something I was about to tell you when Rose came."

"What?" Charlotte asked. The word came out pinched and breathless because her heart had almost stopped beating.

"That it's you I want to be with, Charlotte. You. No one else. I want to be with you always." Lifting his right arm, his good arm, he crushed her to him with such force that all the air went out of her lungs.

All of the memories of the past, all the hurts and misunderstandings, were pushed from her mind. In their place was only an empty space, a space waiting to be filled. "Oh, Juan," she said. She turned her face up to his and kissed him. When she pulled away, she saw that she'd made his face muddy.

"What?" he asked, seeing the laughter in her eyes.

"Here," she said, wiping the mud away with her fingertips. "I seem to have gotten mud all over you."

Juan smiled. "That's what I like about you, Charlotte," he said. "Even your kisses are unpredictable."

He was tired, she could tell. The effort of moving from his bed to the doorway and back again, of laughing and talking and kissing, had exhausted him. Without saying anything more, she got him back into bed.

"Don't you want to change your clothes?" he asked.

Charlotte shook her head. "I just want to sit here with you."

"That mud will dry all over you," he said worriedly.

"It can wait," she said. Reaching out, she took his hand. Her eyes were shining a soft, luminous green. *Like the green of spring leaves*, Juan thought before he fell asleep.

When Luz came in an hour later, she found Charlotte still sitting, holding Juan's hand. She knew without asking that something special had happened.

Chapter Ten

George Harmon was gone for more than a week. When he came home, he had news of the rustlers.

"It is a man named Kincaid," Charlotte's father told Roberto Ortiz. By this time Juan was on his feet again. He no longer spent the days in bed, and just that morning he and Charlotte had gone for a walk together. Leaning forward, he listened with his father. "You weren't the only ones whose cattle were stolen. To the west other small ranchers were bothered too."

"Where's Kincaid now?" Juan asked. "In jail?"

George Harmon shook his head, his face grim. "No, he's still free. But he won't be for long. The Texas Rangers are leading a volunteer company to search for him. I'm going with them. We leave next week."

"Then I will go also," Roberto Ortiz said.

"And I," Juan added.

"*No!*" Until that moment Charlotte had been silent. Now everyone turned to look at her. "You're still recovering, Juan."

"I will be well enough by next week, Charlotte."

There was a look of warning in Juan's dark eyes, but Charlotte didn't see it. "Are you crazy? Are you out of your mind? A week ago, no one knew if you were going to live or die. Now, just like that, you're going to go riding off with the Texas Rangers. You can't, Juan. I won't let you."

The second the words were out of her mouth, she knew she'd said the wrong thing. *I won't let you.* Juan's brows drew together and his mouth settled into a firm line. Discreetly George Harmon and Roberto Ortiz and Luz all found reasons to leave the two alone together.

"You must never tell me what I can and cannot do, *querida*."

His voice was so quiet that Charlotte looked up at him in surprise. Perhaps he wasn't angry after all. But one glance at his face told her that he was. "But Juan, I—"

Juan walked to where she stood and put his arms around her. "Hush," he said firmly, drawing her to him. "I am going to go, Charlotte, with my father and your father and the Rangers. It is my duty to go. You must not argue with me about it."

Why? Charlotte wanted to ask. *Don't I have anything to say about this at all?* She didn't want to argue with Juan, not when she'd come so close to losing him forever. With great difficulty she silenced her thoughts and let herself be taken in his arms. But, in a corner of her mind, a worrisome thought gnawed at her happiness. This wasn't the way it was supposed to be. She was standing in his arms, his hand stroking her hair, but their spirits were sharply divided. If Juan was going to insist on making all the decisions,

decisions that affected both of them, sooner or later it would pull them apart.

This time, Juan, Charlotte thought. *This time, because I love you, I will say nothing. But please, God, don't let anything happen to him. Please.*

When Cleve and Buck learned that Juan was going with the volunteers, they insisted on going along as well. The following week, just hours after the men rode away, the women they'd left behind—Charlotte, Teyah, Maggie, and Lavinia—sat on Cielo Hermoso's wide veranda staring at the sunset.

"If Buck gets shot," Maggie said, setting her glass of lemonade down sharply, "I'll kill him myself when he gets home."

It was funny, but Charlotte didn't laugh. She knew exactly how Maggie felt. It was strange, she thought. She and Maggie and Teyah had grown up in different circumstances; they were as different from each other as one wildflower was different from another. But each one knew what the others were feeling. They knew because they were in love.

"I told George he was too old for such goings-on," Lavinia commented, "but he wouldn't listen. Charlotte, now I know where you get that stubborn streak of yours from."

Charlotte said nothing. She was as worried and upset as the rest of them, but a reassuring thought had just come into her mind, a thought that made the corners of her mouth lift in a smile. Rose Fontaine. No one had seen her all week. She hadn't been back to La Jota once since the day she and Charlotte had fought each other in the mud.

Well, thought Charlotte, *at least I don't have to worry about her anymore*. Compared to dealing with Rose Fontaine, riding with the Rangers didn't seem half so dangerous as it had a few minutes ago.

Juan, with the Rangers and the other men, rode after the outlaw named Kincaid. The trail took them northwest, into a part of Texas Juan hadn't ever seen before.

A day's ride away from La Jota the land shifted subtly. It was still empty and limitless, but now it began to roll softly. As if the land were a giant blanket that someone had shaken gently, Juan thought.

The plants were different too. There was more grass as they rode north, hip-deep and uncut, and it grew thicker and greener than the pasture grass surrounding La Jota. When the wind blew, the grass moved in long, gentle ripples. Juan found himself wishing Charlotte were with him to see it. *When I get home*, he thought, *I will tell her all about it*.

Even as the tension of the chase mounted and they picked up Kincaid's trail, Juan was impressed by the scenery around him. One afternoon, when he and Buck had paused to let their horses drink from a stream, Juan made a wide, sweeping gesture with his hand. "This would be a fine place for a ranch, would it not?"

Buck had pulled off his boots and was wading in the stream, cooling his feet. "What?" he asked, looking up.

"I said, wouldn't this—" There was a popping sound as Juan's words were cut off as cleanly as if a knife had sliced through them. "What the—"

Before he could continue, a second bullet zinged past him. "Kincaid!" he hissed. "Hurry, Buck."

"What about my boots?"

"Leave your boots. We've got to get back to the others. Hurry."

In a matter of seconds the two were on their horses and galloping off at top speed. Bullets buzzed in the air around them but fortunately, none struck home. By the time they caught up with the rest of the men, they were sweating and breathless.

"Kincaid!" Juan shouted, pointing behind him.

The company wheeled in a circle and gave chase, their horses pounding hard across the prairie. The men who'd been chasing Juan and Buck, realizing they were outnumbered, turned to flee. But it was too late. In less than half an hour, the company of volunteer Rangers had surrounded not only Kincaid himself but all five of his rustlers. No one was hurt because Kincaid, seeing that he was outnumbered, gave up without a struggle.

Later that night, watching the bright stars wheel overhead and listening to the snoring men around him, Juan remembered what it was he'd been telling Buck when they were fired on: that this was beautiful land, land suited for ranching. Now that Kincaid had been captured, it seemed even more promising.

Charlotte felt as if she were waiting for a new and important part of her life to begin. She and Juan had had so little time together, so little time to talk about their feelings and plan for the future.

They would have a future together, Charlotte was sure of that. But what kind of a future, she didn't know because she and Juan hadn't had time to talk about it. First, Juan's life had hung in the balance. Then, too soon, he had gone off with the Rangers. Now, while she waited for him to come back, Charlotte's mind raced ahead.

They would get married, of course. Maybe just being in love was enough for Teyah and Maggie, who were younger than she was, but it wasn't going to be enough for her. She wanted a big wedding, a wedding that people would talk about for years afterward. She would go to New Orleans to shop for material, for she wanted a white silk dress with a flowing train, a dress that would take Madame Leblanc months to embroider with tiny seed pearls and rows of lace. Juan would wear his black vaquero's outfit, of course, complete with sparkling conchos. After the ceremony there would be a huge, lavish supper, dancing, and rivers of champagne. Of course, Charlotte thought with a mischievous smile, she would invite Rose Fontaine and her family. It was the very least she could do.

And after the wedding? Charlotte's heart skipped a beat. She and Juan would have their own house, of course, a house he would build for her right here on the vast reaches of Cielo Hermoso. Her father would give them land of their own, she knew he would; and as soon as the house was built, they could devote their attention to raising horses.

It would be wonderful, working side by side with Juan every day, working with him in the stables that they had built together.

A small pinprick of worry jabbed Charlotte. What if Juan had other ideas? What if he wanted her to come live at La Jota? But that was silly, she told herself, it wasn't even practical. Surely Roberto Ortiz could run it by himself. Or, if he could not, she would send a hand from Cielo Hermoso to help. Yes, she and Juan would settle on Cielo Hermoso. It made sense; it was what she wanted. And just as soon as Juan returned, just as soon as this business with Kincaid was finished, she would explain it all to him. Then, for both of them, life would begin again.

"Father?" It was the middle of the night. By tomorrow at this time they would be home. Thinking of this, Juan had been unable to sleep. "Father?" he called again, his voice just loud enough to be heard. "Are you asleep?"

Roberto Ortiz stirred in the blankets next to his son. "What is it, Juan?"

"I wish to talk to you, Father."

Roberto Ortiz's heart thudded once, like a drum. Somehow he had known this was coming. He had sensed all day that something was on his son's mind. "It is important, I take it," he said.

"It is." Juan paused, glad that he could not see his father's face in the darkness. He hadn't thought that this would be easy, but it was proving even more difficult than he'd imagined. "I have been thinking, Father."

"Yes?"

"This land out here, there is so much of it, so much waiting to be claimed. Compared to it, La Jota seems—"

"Small?" his father interrupted.

"Yes," Juan admitted. "La Jota will always be small, Father, because the land surrounding it is owned by others. But out here we—" Juan saw his father's shadow jerk in the darkness.

"We?" Roberto Ortiz questioned. "I would never leave La Jota, Juan, you must know that."

Juan was silent. It was exactly what he'd feared. His father did not understand. His father could not see that, as long as they stayed on La Jota, they would forever be small ranchers.

Just a few days ago the idea of leaving La Jota would have shocked him too. But riding north with the Rangers had opened new doors for him. The land he saw here had a special appeal to him. It was young, like he was, and full of dreams. Together, Juan thought, he and the land could grow. Together they could build something special. But his father's silence sent those dreams crashing into the dust.

"I would never leave La Jota, Juan," his father repeated, breaking the silence, "but that doesn't mean that you could not."

"What?" Juan propped himself on one elbow to listen. "What are you saying, Father?"

Now it was Roberto Ortiz who had difficulty speaking. "I am saying, Juan, that each man must have his own dream. La Jota is special to me because it belonged to my father once, long ago before *los Americanos* came. That is why it was so important to me to get it back; that is why it doesn't matter to me whether it is large or small, whether it supports one cow or one thousand. It is La Jota, it is ours again, and that is what matters."

"Of course," Juan agreed. "I love La Jota as much as you do, Father."

"*Sí*, I know. But perhaps you are meant to have another dream, a bigger dream, a dream of this land."

Juan squinted, looking out into the shadowy darkness. Large, shaggy silhouettes of live oaks rose up in the distance, their tops brushing the star-bright sky. "What if I did have such a dream, Father?" he asked slowly.

"If you did . . . well, a man must follow his own dreams, no?"

A man must follow his own dreams. His father was telling him, giving him permission, to strike out on his own.

"Thank you, Father," Juan murmured, not trusting his emotion-filled voice to say more.

Roberto Ortiz lay back down. "*De nada*, Juan. Think nothing of it." He glanced across at his son, then rolled on his back so that he was looking straight up at the stars. He'd always known this moment would come, when Juan would need to break away, but he hadn't expected it to come so soon.

Juan, like his father, lay looking at the stars. They seemed to sparkle with special brilliance, full of hope and promises for the future. In his mind's eye, Juan pictured a ranch house and endless pastures; he pictured cattle, sleek horses, and cowhands who were brave and loyal. And, most of all, he pictured Charlotte standing by his side.

He smiled to himself. Charlotte would be surprised when he told her. He hadn't even proposed to her yet, not properly anyway; but he knew there was an understanding between them, an understanding as deep as their love. Charlotte was probably already planning their wedding, probably already planning her life with him at La Jota. Well, he would give her something better than La Jota. He would give her a ranch of her own, a ranch that, someday, would be as prosperous as Cielo Hermoso itself.

Charlotte would be surprised when he told her, but she would get over her surprise quickly. Juan had no doubt of that. She loved him, just as he loved her, and because she loved him, his dream would become her dream as well. It was all as simple as that.

Chapter Eleven

Charlotte stared at Juan, green eyes wide with disbelief. "What are you saying, Juan?"

"That the land I saw to the north of here, the land I rode through when we went after Kincaid, is beautiful. It will make a fine ranch."

"But we don't need a ranch," Charlotte replied with a toss of her head. "We have Cielo Hermoso."

"Cielo Hermoso?" Juan asked.

"Yes, Cielo Hermoso. It's my home, Juan. It always will be. And, after we marry, it will be your home as well."

"No."

Juan's voice was so low that Charlotte wasn't sure she'd heard correctly. "What?"

"No," Juan repeated. "I love you, Charlotte, I want us to marry, but we must have a place of our own. A man must stand on his own feet. Surely you know that."

"I don't know anything of the sort!" Charlotte replied, her temper flaring.

Juan's face remained serious. "Well, you know it now, *querida*. I intend to stand on my own feet."

Over the top of Juan's shoulder Charlotte could see the new stables standing white and green in the March sunshine. The sight of the stables fueled her temper. "What about our stables?" she exploded. "Do you expect me just to walk away from them? Just to give them up? What do you think I've been working for all this time?"

Angrily she turned away from him. With a swiftness that took her breath away, Juan seized her elbow and drew her back to him. Before she could draw away in protest, Juan pulled her to him and kissed her. "Is that what you worked for, Charlotte?" he whispered fiercely. "A barn? Some planks of wood? Or was it this?" Before she could reply, he kissed her again. A kiss that, this time, she returned. "It is what we have built between us, Charlotte, that truly matters."

"But—" Charlotte felt torn, torn between Juan and Cielo Hermoso, torn between his wishes and her own. Part of her realized that he was right. He was the kind of man who needed his own dream, his own achievements. But another part of her, an even bigger part, was afraid to leave Cielo Hermoso. It was her home, her world. Never until this moment had she even considered leaving it.

"Say you will come, Charlotte," Juan was coaxing. "Say you will at least come with me and see the land. Just for a visit. And if you do not like it—" Juan stopped abruptly. He was certain that, once Charlotte saw the land, she would love it as much as he did. "I'm going next week to see it again. At least come look at it."

"All right," Charlotte agreed grudgingly. "I will look at it." *But,* she added silently, *I won't like it. I'll never like any place as much as Cielo Hermoso.*

* * *

George Harmon liked Juan Ortiz. He'd come to know both Juan and his father better during the search for Kincaid, and his respect for both men had grown. That didn't mean, however, that he was prepared to let Charlotte go off alone with Juan.

"But I love Juan, Papa," Charlotte protested. "And he loves me."

"I know the two of you love each other, it's easy to see. And all the more reason not to let you go, then," her father replied. "You know what I mean, Charlotte."

Splashes of color appeared on Charlotte's cheeks. "I know what you mean but . . ." Charlotte fell silent, the gears and wheels in her mind clicking rapidly. She'd promised Juan to go look at the new land, and she was determined to keep that promise. "What about a chaperon?" she asked. "We'll take a chaperon."

"Who?" George Harmon asked. "Luz?"

The thought of her maid grumbling along on horseback made Charlotte smile. "Well, maybe not Luz." She paused and thought. "How about Cleve?" she asked. "He's just like a brother to me, Papa, you know he is. He wouldn't let anything happen to me."

George Harmon considered. "If Cleve goes along," he said slowly, "it might be all right."

"Wonderful!" Charlotte said impulsively.

"I'm not so sure."

"Oh, Papa, we'll only be gone a few days. And Cleve . . . you said just last week there's no one you trust more. Please?"

George Harmon looked at his daughter. "This is very important to you, isn't it?"

"Yes, Papa."

There was a moment, a long, agonizing moment of silence as George Harmon thought the matter over. If it were anyone but Cleve going along, he'd never allow it. But Cleve, quiet and levelheaded and protective, would see that nothing unusual went on.

"All right," he consented at last, and Charlotte impulsively flung her arms around him. Usually the gesture pleased him. Today, for some reason, it caused a lump to rise in his throat. He felt dangerously close to losing her, his Charlotte, and there was nothing he could do about it.

Long after she'd dismounted, Charlotte still felt the jolting rhythm of the horse beneath her. Never had she ridden so long or so far in one day. She'd told Juan her body might never recover. Juan had laughed in reply, but he had also hurried to bring her fresh, cool water from a nearby stream.

It was their second night out. Last night they had come across a cabin owned by a young man named Harold Walden and his wife. Without the slightest hesitation the Waldens had invited them to supper and insisted they stay the night. That was the Texas way: When strangers came to your home, you opened your doors to them.

At sunup, after a hearty breakfast, the Waldens had sent them on their way. They hadn't come across another ranch or farm since then. In fact, they hadn't seen a single human being all day long, only mile after mile of gently rolling hills, hills covered with soft spring grass and drifts of brightly colored wildflowers. Now they'd stopped to make camp for the night.

"You mean we're going to sleep here?" Charlotte asked, surprise lifting her eyebrows.

"*Sí,*" Juan replied with a vigorous nod. "Where else, *querida*?"

"But . . . but, it's so *empty,*" Charlotte protested, "and uncomfortable. I'll never be able to sleep."

Juan grinned. "You will see, Charlotte." Working quickly, he pulled several long, straight wooden poles from the saddlepacks and drove them into the ground. Then, unfurling a length of canvas sheeting, he draped the cloth expertly over the poles and pulled it taut, anchoring it to the ground with pegs. The finished result was a tent. "For you," Juan told her. "Cleve and I will sleep outside, to guard you."

"Oh, Juan." Charlotte moved close to him and put her arms around his neck. Cleve had gone off in search of firewood. She and Juan were alone on the whispering prairies. "I wish the tent were for you and me."

It was a bad thing to suggest, she knew it was, but she couldn't resist. She loved him so much.

"Cleve would never approve," Juan said with a smile. "And neither would I."

"Juan! Charlotte! Come see this!" It was Cleve, shouting and motioning to them from the edge of a cottonwood thicket.

"What is it?" Charlotte called back.

But Cleve, without another word, turned and disappeared into the fringe of trees.

Their curiosity aroused, Charlotte and Juan followed him through the sunlight and shadows. It was a hot day, for summer came early to the prairies, and Charlotte found herself growing warm. After a few moments they came to a narrow stream. Cleve walked along the stream bank and they followed him to a place where, suddenly, the stream widened to form a pond of fresh, bubbling water.

"Looks pretty inviting, doesn't it?" Cleve called. Charlotte watched as her stepbrother pulled off his shirt and boots and waded into the water. "Come on in," he shouted, splashing drops of water at them.

Juan, laughing, was quick to join in. Following Cleve's lead, he quickly stripped off his shirt and boots and, wearing only pants, dove in.

Now Charlotte was standing alone on the bank. "Aren't you coming in?" Cleve asked.

Charlotte swallowed. The water looked cool and inviting, but she was frightened. She had never done anything like this. "What's gotten into you, Cleve?" she asked, a crackle of annoyance in her voice. "Papa would never approve of this. You know he wouldn't."

"We're not doing anything wrong, Charlotte," her stepbrother replied. "Nothing to get arrested for, anyway."

Juan, finding his footing on the bottom of the pond, sensed what the real problem was. "You don't know how to swim, do you, Charlotte?" he asked, wading forward.

"N-no," Charlotte admitted reluctantly.

Juan smiled. "Well, we can take care of that." Reaching a wet, dripping hand toward her, he gestured for Charlotte to join him.

Charlotte drew back. "I couldn't," she said.

"Of course you can, *querida*," Juan coaxed.

Charlotte looked at Juan and at the frothy, bubbly water. It was ridiculous even to think about it. She might swallow mouthfuls of water. She might sink and go under. But the water was there before her, cool and tantalizing.

"Just a second!" she cried, reaching for the buttons that fastened her blouse. A minute later, dressed only in chemise and petticoats, she was splashing into the water, her heart pounding with excitement.

"Slowly, *querida*," Juan warned.

But Charlotte didn't listen. Anxious to reach his outstretched hand, exhilarated by the cool water lapping against her, she plunged forward. Her foot slipped against the bottom and she went under, gulping water in, breathing it into her lungs. She felt a hand drawing her to the surface.

"Are you all right?" Juan asked.

Charlotte coughed. She blinked water from her eyes. She tossed her hair, blond and dripping, behind her shoulders.

"Are you all right?" Juan asked again.

Both Juan and Cleve were watching her, waiting for her answer. "Of course I am," she said. "I just lost my balance."

Juan smiled proudly. "Good. Now, *querida*, I will teach you how to swim."

At first Charlotte wasn't sure she could do it. Wading into the pond was one thing, but learning to swim was another. Yet when Juan showed her how to pull the water back with her hands, how to kick to stay afloat, she found her fear vanishing. Setting her chin stubbornly, she set out to follow Juan's instructions. She went under several

times, swallowing mouthfuls of water each time,
and once Juan had to catch her because she was
headed directly for a fallen log. But eventually
she managed to stay afloat on her own. When that
happened, a feeling of excitement raced through
her body. Maybe this is what Juan means about
living in a new land, she thought. Maybe it has
something to do with feeling like this.

Her mind was so busy thinking that she
forgot to take a stroke, and when her arms forgot
to take a stroke, her feet forgot to kick. Before she
knew it, she was going under again, with water
rushing into her mouth and lungs. Sputtering,
she touched bottom with her feet and turned to
glare at Juan. "Why didn't you grab me?" she
asked. "I suppose you were just going to let me
drown."

He shook his head. "You know what to do
now, *querida*. You don't need me to help you
every time you get a mouthful of water."

Suddenly Charlotte was annoyed. She liked
feeling free and independent, but she liked
feeling the other way, too: She liked having Juan
rescue her. "It'd serve you right if I *did* drown,"
she mumbled, wading upstream against the
current. Hoping to make him feel guilty, she
coughed loudly.

But Juan only smiled. "I love you, *querida*,"
he said. "And I am very proud of you."

That night, in the tent Juan had made,
Charlotte lay awake for a long time. Thoughts
swirled through her mind like shooting stars,
thoughts that came from different directions and
had different meanings.

Juan was right about the land, it *was* beautiful. She loved the way the long grass rippled in

the wind, loved the masses of purple and red-orange wildflowers that grew everywhere. But beautiful as the land was, it was also empty. There wasn't a cabin for miles around; and the closest town was Collinsville, one narrow, muddy street joined by another narrow, muddy street. It wasn't at all like San Antonio, with its many shops and plazas. Out here there would be no neighbors, not at first, anyway. There would be no festive balls, no daylong barbecues, no Madame Leblanc to make gowns for her. Out here she wouldn't even need gowns.

Charlotte bit her lip. There was something else that bothered her, too, something that was more important than all the gowns and all the parties in the world. It was Juan. It was Juan, and as much as Juan, it was herself.

Charlotte remembered the way Juan had looked at her when she had jumped into the pond beside him. She remembered the smile on his face as he'd watched her conquer the water. Pride had showed in his eyes, pride and love. Is that how it would be between them out here? Charlotte wondered. Would Juan always be pushing her, expecting her to do things she had never done before?

She remembered the sweet, exultant feeling learning to swim had given her. She enjoyed that feeling, yes, but could she do it again? Could she give up the safe, sure life of Cielo Hermoso for a life of risks and hazards?

Charlotte turned restlessly in her blankets. She loved Juan, there was no question of that. But whether she loved him enough to follow him into a new and uncertain life, that was another matter entirely.

Chapter Twelve

The next morning they left camp to explore the land on the other side of the river. "It's just more pastureland," Charlotte grumbled, but Juan wanted her to see it nevertheless.

Cleve, intrigued by the vastness of the scenery, rode ahead of them at a swift pace. As he galloped off, Charlotte could feel her own horse straining to be in motion, but she held the mare carefully in check. She wasn't about to show such reckless excitement, not with Juan watching her every move and gesture.

"Isn't this a beautiful land, *querida*?" he asked eagerly, riding alongside her.

"Especially these bugs," Charlotte replied dryly, slapping at the insects that swirled before her face. "I don't know where I've seen more of them."

Juan laughed, confident that Charlotte could not ignore forever the beauty surrounding them. He was right, though she wasn't yet ready to tell him so. As they rode along, the land that had seemed endless and empty took on a life of its own. Birds dipped and soared in the turquoise sky above them, and jackrabbits bounded through the quivering grass. Once a huge butterfly lighted on her hand and rode along for several seconds before stretching its velvety wings and fluttering away.

Oh, Juan, this is beautiful land, but can I follow you here? Can I give up Cielo Hermoso and everything it stands for to be with you? Am I that strong?

Charlotte's brow furrowed as she pondered alternatives. Always before, her course in life had been perfectly clear, every decision and every choice mapped out neatly. School, parties, dinner at seven, a fitting with Madame Leblanc, shopping in San Antonio with Lavinia, going to New Orleans for shoes and hats and leather gloves. With Juan there were no clear routines to follow. Everything was different. That was what she loved about him, but that was also what frightened her.

She looked toward the horizon, a strip of earth as wild and uncertain as her future with Juan seemed to be. Suddenly she saw something moving there. No, she decided, her eyes were playing tricks on her. There was nothing in this landscape except for herself, Juan, and their horses. Even Cleve had disappeared, riding so far to the west that he'd vanished from sight.

She rode a few more steps and looked again, this time shading her eyes with the palm of her hand. There was something there. At first it looked like a thin brown line above the grass. Then, as she stared, the line changed shape before her eyes, surging forward, trampling the grass beneath it.

"Juan!" The instant the word left her lips, the first sounds reached them, a low and ponderous rumble.

Juan's head jerked toward the horizon. "Buffalo!" he shouted.

Charlotte nodded. Panic gripped her heart. The buffalo were running quickly, stampeding across the open sweep of prairie. As the animals spilled over the horizon, what had seemed like a thin brown line at first stretched out to become a blanket, a blanket that stretched as far as she could see!

"They'll trample us to death!" she cried.

Juan was already wheeling his horse around. "We'll run for it," he told her, shouting to make himself heard above the rumbling sound.

Charlotte jerked her horse's reins, and she and Juan set out at a dead gallop. Her heart was pounding, and her stomach felt as if it were dropping through the earth itself. Never in her entire life had she been so terrified. With a quick backward glance over her shoulder, she saw the tide of animals surging toward them.

This ought to show Juan what a dangerous land this is! she thought fiercely. *Maybe now he'll understand why it's not a good idea to move here. Why, something like this could happen any time at all. We could move here and be killed, trampled, before we even get a house built!*

The satisfaction of knowing that Juan would realize this almost made up for the terror she felt. Glancing sideways, she looked at Juan, hoping to see a guilt-stricken look on his face. Instead he was smiling! She was so startled that she brought her horse to an abrupt halt.

"What are you doing, Charlotte?" he called back to her.

"Why are you smiling?" she shouted.

He looked at her as if she'd lost her mind. "Do you want to be trampled? What's wrong with you, Charlotte?"

She looked over her shoulder long enough to see the shaggy, boulderlike heads of the buffalo. Sunlight glinted off their white horns. "We can't outrun them," she shouted angrily. "We're going to be trampled, and it's all your fault!"

"No, we aren't. We can outrun them if we hurry."

Charlotte didn't move. There was no time to argue. In one swift movement Juan rode back to her and slapped her horse's rump. The horse took off so quickly that Charlotte almost lost her seat. *I suppose he'll think that's funny too!* she thought angrily.

They said nothing more for several minutes. Only when they'd ridden beyond the far western ridge, only when the enormous herd had thundered by, did they speak again.

"It's safe now," Juan said. Grinning, he lifted up his hands to help her down off her horse.

All the fear she'd just felt came flooding back to her. "No, it isn't safe," she snapped. "It's never safe out here. We could have died back there. I could have been trampled to death. And you thought it was all a joke! Don't deny it, Juan. I looked at you and you were smiling. *Smiling!*" Suddenly she was furious with him. How could he have risked her life, and his own, so casually? "Don't you care about me at all, Juan? How could you place me in such danger?" Ignoring his outstretched hands, she dismounted by herself.

"Maybe it was a little bit dangerous, *querida*. But only a little bit. I told you we could outrun them. There would have been no danger at all if you hadn't stopped your horse." He took her by the shoulders and stared for a long moment into her eyes, unable to keep a smile from forming on his lips. "Admit it, *querida*, it was exciting, was it not? A little bit dangerous, but very, *very* exciting."

It was exciting, she realized. The breathless dash across the prairie, the little thrill she'd felt as they watched, from a distance, as the herd pounded by. But she would never admit that to him. Never.

By the time they got back to camp, Cleve was waiting for them. He had seen the buffalo herd, too, and headed back toward camp.

"Weren't you scared?" Charlotte asked, but Cleve only shook his head. "All I can say, then," she replied, "is that you're as crazy, as loco, as Juan is." And settling herself among a pile of saddle blankets, she began to pout.

A few minutes later Cleve slipped quietly up to Juan. "Is something wrong with Charlotte?" he asked.

Juan shook his head. "Nothing she won't get over."

"Maybe you can iron things out if I leave you alone for a while," Cleve suggested.

Juan smiled. "Maybe we can. Thanks, *amigo*."

"Good luck," Cleve replied with a grin, reaching for his horse's reins.

After Cleve had gone, Juan waited a few minutes. Then he went over and sat down beside Charlotte. "How do you feel, *querida*?"

Well, this is more like it, Charlotte thought. She covered her eyes with her hand. "I think I'm going to be sick," she said dramatically.

Juan's laugh filled the air. That was when Charlotte's foot slipped and she kicked him. But that only made him laugh harder. "You see?" he asked. "You are not sick at all. You are stronger than you think, *querida*."

Charlotte dropped her hand. It was no use trying to pretend with him. All of the ploys and tactics she used on other boys were useless where Juan was concerned.

Juan got to his feet and offered her his hand. "Come, *querida*," he said. "You cannot sit here all night."

She took his hand and let herself be drawn to her feet. When she was standing, Juan did not let go of her hand. Instead he drew her close to him and, with his other hand, began stroking her hair. "You are brave, Charlotte, and strong. Stronger and braver than you know, and I love you very much."

"Oh, Juan, I love you too, it's just that—"

"Shh," he said, stopping her words with a kiss.

Charlotte returned his kiss. She sighed and leaned against him. When would they be married? It seemed so far away, and there were so many obstacles to overcome before then. The question of where to live still loomed between them, even larger after today. He'd said he loved her, but did that mean that he was willing to abandon his dream of starting a new ranch out here on the fringe of the world?

Maybe we'll never be married, she thought; the idea sent a chill of alarm racing through her.

"Oh, Juan," she sighed, "I wish we were married. I wish we were home."

"We are home," he whispered gently.

Involuntarily she tensed in his arms. "What do you mean?"

"I meant to keep this as a surprise," he said, looking down at her. "I meant to wait to tell you until you were more used to the idea, until you came to love this land as much as I do."

"Tell me what?" she asked, a suspicion forming in her mind.

"This *is* our home, our land."

"*What?*" She jerked away from him, unwilling to believe what she had just heard.

Juan's voice remained gentle. "The minute I saw this land, I knew it was meant for me, for *us*. Last week I went to the land claim office and put a claim on it. It took every cent I had, we will be poor at first, but—"

"You spent your money on this?" she asked, opening her arms to gesture toward the empty horizons. "And you expect me to come live here with you?"

"I would live here with no one else, *querida*. This is to be *our* home."

"But you didn't even ask me!" she cried, her voice shaking with anger. "You say you love me, Juan, but you never even think of me. Today you almost got me killed by wild buffalo, and now you buy this land without even talking to me about it!"

Everything was going wrong. Juan was hurt; he'd meant this to be a gift for her, but Charlotte didn't see that. There was only room in her mind for her own anger. She whirled away from him and started walking up the hill that sheltered their camp. Her skirt whipped and snapped in the gusty spring breeze. At the top of the hill she stopped and stared off across the empty horizon. The grass rustled as Juan came up behind her.

"This is where I mean our house to be, *querida*," he said softly. "From here you can see the country in every direction. Look, you can even see the pond where we went swimming yesterday."

Charlotte did not say anything. Nor did she turn to see the view of the pond. Her shoulders rose and fell like bird wings, she was so angry. Hadn't Juan heard a word she said? Wasn't he going to pay any attention to her feelings at all?

"You are being unfair, *querida*," he said. "You are being unfair to me and to yourself. You have a feeling for this land, too, I know you do. You are just too stubborn to admit it."

With that he turned and started down the hill. Charlotte was left standing alone. Juan's words stung. Besides, in her heart, she knew they were true.

He's the stubborn one, she thought, burying Juan's words in her own anger. *How could I ever have thought I loved him? How could I ever have planned to marry him?*

With a jerk of her chin she turned and started back down the hill. When she reached the campfire, she said, "I want to go back, Juan. Tomorrow morning. I want you to take me back to Cielo Hermoso."

But the next morning, when they rode away from the camp, she felt as if she were leaving a little piece of herself behind.

Chapter Thirteen

Charlotte and Juan exchanged hardly more than a dozen words on the way home. It was as if each one of them was hiding behind a wall of pride, a wall neither one of them wanted to be the first to drop. As if to make the evening even glummer, a gray, misty drizzle settled over the land. Later that night Juan brought an extra sheet of canvas to Charlotte's tent. "To keep off the rain," he said, shaking out the canvas and covering the little tent with it.

"Thank you," Charlotte said stiffly.

"*De nada*," Juan answered.

His voice was without its usual self-assured lilt, but Charlotte didn't notice. She was lost in her own thoughts.

He doesn't understand how I feel at all, Charlotte brooded. Suddenly she found herself thinking of her half sister. Love seemed to come so easily to Teyah; never once had she witnessed between Teyah and Cleve the kind of battles and misunderstandings that took place between herself and Juan. It didn't seem to matter to Teyah that Cleve made the plans for both of them. *But it matters to me!* Charlotte thought passionately. *It matters and he knows it! Maybe he's right about the land, about starting a new ranch, but buying the land—that's something we should have decided together.*

Self-righteous anger bubbled inside her. It was easy to forget that she had made up her mind for herself, easy to forget that she had almost decided to tell Juan she would join him in his dreams. It was easy to forget, too, that he had meant the land to be a surprise for her, a gift that would symbolize their future together. Reminding herself of those facts cooled her anger and clouded her feelings with doubts. And if there was one thing Charlotte didn't like, it was uncertainty.

When they finally reached Cielo Hermoso, Juan helped her down off her horse. "We need to talk, *querida*. I will be back tomorrow morning, after we have both had a good night's sleep." She nodded, not quite able to meet his eyes. "Charlotte?"

She looked up to find him staring intently at her. "Yes?"

"This is very important for us."

There was no compromise in his voice. None. "I know," she said.

He reached out to stroke her cheek. "Sleep well, *querida*."

"I will."

She was proud of herself. She managed to keep her tears to herself until she was alone in her room.

There was going to be a party at Cielo Hermoso. It was a new tradition, one that Maggie McNeill had started. After her first cattle drive she'd given a party to celebrate. Now it was Cielo

Hermoso's turn to celebrate the end of the spring drives.

Because Cielo Hermoso was Cielo Hermoso, the party this year was going to be bigger and grander than ever. The celebration was still four days away, but already workmen were building a wooden dance floor at the foot of the wide, sweeping lawn that stretched away from the house. Lanterns with colored glass were being filled with oil so that, when the proper time came, they would be ready to cast red and blue and golden lights on the dancers. Barbecue pits were being dug and, in the kitchen, huge pots of dried beans were being soaked.

Everyone in the county was coming. Even Rose Fontaine, who, Charlotte heard, had recently become engaged to one of the Richter boys. Charlotte wondered if Juan would come too. She tried to picture herself dancing in his arms, tried to picture her father and Juan's father standing together to announce their engagement to everyone.

Well, it would all be settled soon enough. Juan was coming this morning. This morning they would talk. This morning her future would be decided.

Charlotte smiled to herself. After she had had a good night's sleep everything looked more hopeful to her. Surely Juan would see his mistake, would see that it was important to make decisions together. As soon as he apologized, as he surely would, she would forgive him. Then everything would be perfect.

Her thoughts took wings. Juan would come to the party and then, with her to guide him, he would see the charm and beauty of Cielo Hermoso. It would be a night of magic, a night of new beginnings and new understandings. If he saw Cielo Hermoso through her eyes, he would love it as much as she did. Perhaps he would even change his mind about wanting to live there.

Charlotte plucked a fresh flower from a vase and arranged it in her hair. It was possible that Juan would want to live at Cielo Hermoso after all. She tried to think of something she had wanted very badly and never gotten. There was nothing. Not one single thing. In her whole life she had gotten everything she really wanted. She might get this too.

By the time Luz told her that Juan was waiting in the parlor, she was full of confidence again. Her smile was so bright that at first Juan was startled. Then he smiled back at her. So, he thought, she has come to her senses. She has seen how foolish it is to pout, just because things did not happen exactly the way she expected them to.

They walked outside, past the people who were busily preparing for the party and far, far past the stables they had built together. They walked until there was nothing and no one around them but the land.

Juan stooped down, plucked an indigo-colored flower called a bluebonnet, and gave it to her. "I am glad to see you smiling again, *querida*," he said.

She waited. The apology would come now. She was certain of it. Instead he took her hand. "Just to see you, *querida*, makes me . . ."

"Makes you what?" she prompted.

"It's hard to explain," he answered. "It makes me want to build things, to start our lives.

It makes me want to start our ranch now, today, even though I know I have to wait until the end of the week."

Charlotte stiffened. "What do you mean, the end of the week?"

Juan had thought it all out. He had lain awake most of the night thinking, planning. He knew Charlotte better than she knew herself, he was sure of that. If he waited for her to make up her mind, she would take forever, torn between the luxury of Cielo Hermoso and her love for him. In time their love would dwindle, not grow, until there was nothing left. It was better to risk everything, he had decided, better to gamble everything on the strength of their love for each other.

"I am going back to our land on Saturday morning. I must start building now, immediately, *querida*, if we are to have a house to move into by autumn. And there must be barns and corrals, too, for the cattle as well as the horses."

"But—" Charlotte felt dizzy. For one long, excruciating moment she thought she was going to be ill. This wasn't at all what she'd expected. *Nothing has changed*, she thought, *nothing, nothing, nothing!*

"But Saturday's the day of the party," she continued lamely. "I . . . I counted on you being there. . . ." There was no way to explain the other things she'd counted on.

Juan studied her face. *I can't believe this is happening*, he told himself, *I can't believe that she wants a party and a new dress as much as she wants me, as much as she wants love!*

"A party?" he asked, his voice sharper than he meant it to be. He grasped her firmly by the shoulders and looked deep into her eyes. "Haven't you been to enough parties to last a lifetime, *querida*? Aren't there more important things to do with one's life?"

She bit her lip. The heavy feeling in her stomach hardened into a ball of lead. Couldn't he understand her just a little bit? Just this once? She tried to talk, to find words to explain her tangled feelings to him, but she couldn't. For the first time in her life she couldn't think of a thing to say.

"I am going back to the land to begin a cabin on Saturday. If you love me, if you wish for us to have a life together, you must tell me." He paused, hoping that she would speak, but she looked stubbornly down, her gaze focused on a single button on his shirt.

"Very well," he said, letting go of her, as deeply disappointed as she was. "Very well. If you change your mind, *querida*, let me know. If not, I will know that there is nothing to come back here for. Nothing." Turning, he walked away from her.

Charlotte could not sleep. There was no reason to sleep, she told herself. Just as there was no reason to get up, to smile, to think of the future. There was no reason to do anything. Not when her heart ached. Not when her heart felt as if burning coals had been heaped onto it.

Restless, she got up and treaded lightly down the stairs. A pale beam of light from the dining room fell across the carpet. Charlotte followed the light and found her father seated at the end of the table, ledgers and account books spread out before him. He often worked late into the night, enjoying the silence and the safe, secure feeling of the big ranch slumbering around him.

"Papa?" Charlotte crossed the threshold and padded into the dining room on bare feet.

Her father looked up. He'd been worried about her all day, had wanted to ask her what was the matter, but Lavinia had stopped him. "It has something to do with Juan," his wife had said. "When Charlotte's ready, she'll tell us what it is."

Now, seeing his daughter's troubled expression, he couldn't hold himself back. "What's wrong, Little Charlie?"

Little Charlie. He hadn't used that nickname for years, nor that gentle, understanding tone of voice. *If only we could go back in time!* she thought suddenly. *If only we could start over!* Everything had been so simple then. Then, there had been no difficult decisions to make.

Charlotte pulled back a chair and sat down beside her father. A tear slipped down her cheek, followed by another and another. "Oh, Papa!" she said, burying her face in her hands. "Oh, Papa, I've made such a mess of my life!"

George Harmon didn't know what to do at first. For years he'd left the care of his daughter to others: first to Luz and the other maids and now, in the last two years, to Lavinia. But none of them were around now. He was alone with his daughter in the great dining room. Laying down the pen he'd been balancing accounts with, he stroked Charlotte's thick, golden hair. "Tell me what's wrong, Little Charlie," he said, "maybe we can fix it."

It all tumbled out then, all her anger and confusion, all her hopes and disappointments, all her love for Juan Ortiz.

"You do like him, don't you, Papa?" she asked through her tears. It mattered to her, suddenly, that her father approve of Juan.

George Harmon hesitated. "Yes, Charlotte, I do like him. He's a fine young man." He smiled faintly. "Actually, he's a lot like you. He knows what he wants in life and won't take *no* for an answer. You're like peas in a pod that way, both of you stubborn and determined."

"Oh, no, Papa," Charlotte said in a rush, "I'm not nearly as stubborn as Juan." And then she explained it all to him again, how Juan had claimed the land without asking her, how he expected her to go along with whatever he planned for them. "It's not right, is it, Papa?" she asked.

"Maybe it's not right, Charlotte, but sometimes it's the way men are. When a man loves a woman, he wants to make a whole world for her. I wanted that for your mother. Why, do you know, Charlotte, she followed me out here to this land without even seeing it first? Juan's at least shown you the land."

It shocked Charlotte a little that her father seemed to be taking Juan's side. "Maybe he *has* shown it to me," she said, "but he's never really asked me how I feel about it." She sniffed. "He ought to at least ask me," she said.

"Yes," her father admitted, "he probably should have. But people don't always do what they ought to do. If you do marry Juan, there'll be lots of times when he doesn't do what you want him to, times when you'll think he's just flat out wrong. But there'll be just as many times when he'll think the same thing about you. People who love each other get around those times."

Charlotte didn't reply. She was thinking of her mother, following her father in the wide, empty spaces of Texas, following him to a place she had never even seen before, just because he'd asked her to, just because she loved him. Even with that thought in her head Charlotte wasn't ready to back down. "But I'm right about him asking me, aren't I, Papa? He really should have asked."

George Harmon closed his ledger book and turned down the wick of the lamp. "You can be right, Charlotte, and you can be loved, but sometimes you can't be both at the same time. Suppose you are right. Is it worth losing Juan over?"

The words stayed in her mind long after the light in the oil lamp flickered out.

Charlotte knew, now, what she was going to do. She was going to give in, something she had never done before. She was going to go to Juan and tell him that she loved him, and she was going to tell him that because she loved him, she would follow him anywhere. She would have gone to live with him in China if that was what he'd really wanted.

But being the first one to give in wasn't easy, especially for Charlotte. She put off riding to Juan's for three days, hoping that he would give in first after all, hoping that he would come to her. When he didn't, though, she didn't change her mind. She put on her most dashing riding habit, had her horse saddled, and set off across the plains.

It was Saturday morning, the day of the party, the day Juan had said he was leaving. She'd set out early, picturing the dramatic scene she'd make as she galloped into the yard of La Jota. By this time Juan would have all but given up hope of hearing from her. He would be depressed and dejected, his handsome face dark and sad. But when he saw her riding up to him, when he heard what she had to say, his eyes would glow with their special light. He would smile his flashing smile and whirl her in his arms. She hoped that maybe he would even consent to stay for the party. That was all she asked. Just one night with him at Cielo Hermoso. Then she would follow him to the ends of the earth.

Her heart raced with excitement as she neared La Jota. She was dressed in a handsome navy riding habit with gold trim sewn to look like a soldier's uniform. Her navy hat bore a single canary-colored feather, and there were gold corded laces in her riding boots.

When Juan and I get married, she thought giddily, *I think I'll wear gold silk petticoats under my gown. Then, just when everyone's thinking how proper and polite I look, I'll raise the hem just enough to show it off. Won't people be shocked?*

The idea pleased her and she smiled. Juan would enjoy her brightly colored petticoats more than anyone. That was the kind of life they would live together, a life not at all like anyone else's, a life everyone else thought of as just a little bit shocking.

La Jota was in view now. Someone was in the yard. Juan, Charlotte thought at first, but as she galloped nearer, she saw that it was Juan's father, Roberto Ortiz. *My future father-in-law*, she thought, and a faint flush came to her cheeks.

"*Buenos días*," she called out, using the few words of Spanish she knew. Drawing her horse to a halt, she looked eagerly around the yard. "Where's Juan?"

"Juan?"

The older man looked surprised. *Juan's probably told him about our problems*, Charlotte decided. "Yes, Juan. I must talk to him."

"But Juan is gone, senorita. He left for the new land."

"When?"

"He left last night."

The words struck her like a thunderbolt. *Last night!* He hadn't even waited for her answer. Perhaps he'd never meant to.

Chapter Fourteen

Charlotte could hear music. It came from the foot of the lawn and drifted up to her. She stood in her bare feet, gripping the curtain as she stared from the window of her bedroom, her fingers twisting the heavy gold fringe that bordered the luxurious wine-colored velvet drapery.

On the bed behind her was the dress she'd meant to wear tonight, a dress she'd chosen especially with Juan in mind. It was a deep cream color with a tight-fitting bodice and an off-the-shoulder neckline. Circling that neckline were flounces of black lace. The skirt of the dress was trimmed with ruffled tiers of black lace, and there was a black lace sash as well.

If things had worked out differently, she would be putting on that dress now. She would be slipping her feet into black satin slippers and tapping her toes in time to the drifting music. But things hadn't worked out that way; and now she stood uncertainly, her hair a tangled mass, her clothes crumpled from her having slept in them all day.

Everyone in the house knew there was something dreadfully wrong with her. The maids had glided back and forth in the hallway all afternoon, their voices lowered to a curious whisper. An hour ago Lavinia had knocked on her door to remind her that the party would begin at seven. It was Lavinia's way of reminding her that no matter what had happened between herself and Juan, she was expected to attend the party.

Charlotte wasn't sure what she was going to do. Her face felt hot and puffy from lying on her bed all afternoon. Her nose was red and stuffy from crying. Why she would want to go to a party, she had no idea. And yet, something prompted her to get up off the bed. Maybe it's only habit, she thought, looking at her reflection in the mirror.

There was a rapid knock at the door. Charlotte didn't answer. She couldn't face her stepmother, not just yet. In fact, she wasn't sure she could face anyone.

The knock came again, and a voice. "Charlotte? It's me, Teyah." Slowly Charlotte went to the door and opened it. Teyah hurried in, closing the door behind her. "You look terrible," she said, her eyes sweeping Charlotte from head to toe. "What happened?"

"I don't want to talk about it."

Teyah nodded. She was already dressed for the party herself, her pale blond hair pulled into a gleaming coil that sat on the top of her head like a crown. "Is that what you're wearing?" she asked, glancing at the dress spread across the bed. Then, without waiting for an answer, she reached for the brush that sat on Charlotte's dresser. "We're going to have to work fast," she said.

"Fast for what?"

"The party," Teyah answered. "It's almost time to go down."

Charlotte's mouth settled into a grim line. "I'm not sure I want to go to a party," she said.

"Well, you have to." Teyah sat down on the bed and looked at Charlotte. "I know something happened between you and Juan. But whatever it is, you can fix it, Charlotte. You can work it out between you."

Charlotte shook her head. "Not this time, Teyah. Juan's out of my life for good."

Teyah didn't know what to say. She only knew that sitting up here and brooding all night would do Charlotte no good at all. "Well, if he's out of your life, he's out of your life. But you can't stop living because of it, Charlotte. If you don't come down, everyone will say that Juan Ortiz broke your heart."

Charlotte's chin lifted. "He couldn't break my heart if he tried," she said, a trace of pride showing through her tattered feelings.

Teyah breathed a sigh of relief. "Show them, then," she said.

Charlotte reached for the dress, shaking out its heavy sweep of cascades and ruffles. "I intend to," she said. "Here, hold this while I find my black stockings. I don't know what Luz was thinking of, laying out this dress with white stockings."

Charlotte's resolve carried her out across the lawn to the place where the party was to be held. She walked with the slightly pigeon-toed walk that, she knew, made her skirts sway alluringly. Her deep golden hair was swept up into a rich coil, except for the little wispy curls that danced at her forehead and trailed at the nape of her neck. Her eyes were no longer red, thank goodness, but crying had given them a soft, dewy look.

Charlotte knew that she looked beautiful, maybe even more beautiful than she had looked at Rose Fontaine's ball. But it was a different kind of beauty, not beauty that came from dashing high spirits but a quiet, fragile kind of beauty. She had Juan to thank for that, she knew. It was suffering over him that had brought the haunting expression to her face. Looking in the mirror as Luz had put the finishing touches on her hair, she almost didn't recognize herself.

"What is it, Luz?" she had asked. "Why do I look so different tonight?"

"I think, perhaps, that senorita has grown up," Luz had replied, careful not to mention Juan directly.

So that was it. She was grown up, beautiful and grown up at last, exactly what Juan had wanted. Only Juan was far away. Quickly she pushed the memory of Juan from her mind.

"Charlotte!" She looked up. It was Jim Richter, a young man she'd known since childhood. He was striding toward her on long legs, smiling as he brushed his blond hair back with one hand. "You look beautiful! I haven't seen you for so long, for a while we thought you'd given up parties completely." He took her arm and bent toward her, blue eyes sparkling. "I hope this means you're coming out of retirement!"

Charlotte snapped open the fan that dangled from a black silk cord at her wrist. She raised it, protesting about the spring heat, and looked at Jim over the top of it with dancing green eyes. "I'll consider it," she said. It was all a reflex action, smiling, flirting, showing an interest she didn't begin to feel. But it was better than crying and better than thinking of Juan. Jim Richter, walking along beside her, had no idea of the pain she was in. "Maybe it's time for me to start going to parties again," she said.

"I hope so," Jim laughed. "Parties just haven't been the same without you, Charlotte. Oh, I know Rose Fontaine tried to make a big splash, but she can't hold a candle to you. Besides," he added, "Rose is engaged now." He smiled suddenly. "Promise that you'll dance the first dance with me."

"Of course," she answered.

Now another young man, Keith Eldridge, came up to join them. "If you think you can have Charlotte all to yourself," he challenged, looking at Jim, "you'll have to answer to me."

Charlotte laughed and lifted her free elbow. "Goodness, I *do* have two arms. There's no need to fight over me."

But she enjoyed their lighthearted bantering. It made her feel wanted. *If only Juan were here to see it*, she thought. *Juan*. She had to stop thinking of him. If she didn't, she'd start to fall apart right here under everyone's watchful eyes; and all of the flirting and all of the black lace in the world wouldn't be able to hold her together.

"Who are you eating barbecue with, Charlotte?" Now it was Ed Thompson who'd come to join them, along with his friend Peter Voss.

She looked at the four handsome faces clustered around her. All she could think of was that none of them were Juan and that it didn't matter who she ate with or danced with. It didn't even matter if she ate or danced at all. She smiled and tossed her head. "Settle it among your-selves," she said, and disentangling herself from them, glided off to meet her father's other guests.

It was seeing Teyah and Maggie that was difficult. For Teyah on Cleve's arm and Maggie holding hands with Buck reminded her of every-thing she had lost. Seeing those two happy couples made her think, again, that there was something deeply wrong with her, something that would forever prevent her from falling in love and being happy.

Seeing Charlotte, Maggie left Buck and came over to her. "How are you, Charlotte?" she asked cautiously.

"Oh, I'm fine," Charlotte said, then halted abruptly. "Oh, Maggie, I'm not fine at all. I wish . . . I wish everything were different!" She stopped, biting her lip. If she said more, she'd begin to cry again. And if she began to cry again, she might not be able to stop.

"Things will be different for you someday, Charlotte, I know they will. You deserve to be happy."

The words startled Charlotte. The two girls had grown up together, had been friends because they were the only two girls close to the same age in a ten-mile radius. But they hadn't always liked each other. There had been a time, just a few years ago, when Maggie had thought Charlotte was spoiled and selfish beyond belief. And, of course, Charlotte had been aware of her feelings.

"Do you really mean that, Maggie?"

Maggie looked at her a moment. "Yes, I do. You've changed, Charlotte."

Charlotte smiled, not her flirting smile but a smile that came from her heart. "Thank you, Maggie."

Dusk was falling across the Texas plains, and the lanterns were being lit. Dapples of colored light shone everywhere. Just as dinner was about to be served, a carriage drove up and stopped between two of the brightly flaring torches that had been planted in the ground at wide intervals.

The carriage looked vaguely French, and seeing it, Charlotte realized at once who must be inside. The door opened, and Carl Richter, Jim's older brother, stepped out. Then he held his arm up to help the girl he'd recently become engaged to. A sharp intake of breath rippled through the crowd as Rose Fontaine emerged from the carriage.

She was wearing a dress of dark green silk, a dress so luscious it looked almost edible. The dress's low neckline set off Rose's cream-colored neck and shoulders beautifully, and her dark hair, brushed to perfection, was arranged in rows of long, gleaming curls that trailed down one side of her neck. But most spectacular of all were the jewels. Rubies, a fortune's worth of them, were set in a choker that sparkled at Rose's throat. Interspersed with the rubies were tiny diamonds, diamonds that flashed and danced in the colored lantern light.

No one had ever seen anything quite like it. Many of the people at the party were well-off, and many of them, like Charlotte's father, were building splendid fortunes from the cattle they bred. But all of them, even the Harmons, had a practical streak. They might own fine houses and clothes, they might even allow their daughters to go to New Orleans to shop, but that was as far as it went. Except for a few pearl pins or modest diamond earrings, jewels were unknown to them. And here before them, dripping with rubies like a princess, stood Rose Fontaine.

Charlotte felt her stomach turn, making her feel, for a moment, slightly seasick. She realized at once what Rose was up to—revenge. Weeks ago Charlotte had upstaged Rose at her own party. Now Rose meant to repay her.

There's only one thing wrong, Charlotte thought. *I don't care anymore. She can attract as much attention as she wants. It doesn't matter to me anymore.*

As dinner ended and the music began, Charlotte began to understand the trap she'd made for herself. Everyone was waiting for her to do something. When Carl Richter led Rose out onto the wooden planks for the first dance, there was a whisper of disappointment when Charlotte failed to join in.

"But you promised to dance the first dance with me," Jim Richter protested as the music began and his brother and Rose glided under the lights.

"I know I did," Charlotte apologized, "but I . . . I don't feel very well."

She couldn't tell him how tired she was of it all: of flirting, of competing with girls like Rose, of trying to pretend she was happy when, inside, she was certain she would never be happy again.

Even Rose looked disappointed when Charlotte stayed in the background. She'd been looking forward to the confrontation, had planned to flirt with each and every one of Charlotte's beaus. The fact that she was now engaged wasn't about to stop her. Charlotte Harmon, she'd long ago decided, deserved to be taught a lesson.

As the second dance began, Cleve came up to her. "I'm surprised, Charlotte," he said, studying her with his kind, serious brown eyes.

"About what?"

"You just never struck me as the type to give up."

"Oh, Cleve, please, not you too. I'm so . . ." she gestured at the dance floor with her closed fan, "so sick of all this."

There was silence between them, but only for a moment. Then Cleve spoke again. "There's a lot of people you're letting down, you know. They believe in you, Charlotte, and they're going to be awfully let down if you let Rose get away with this. Your father's one of them. I heard him telling someone that you'd never let someone like Rose be the belle of Cielo Hermoso, not even for one night."

The words sifted through her despair and lodged in her mind. *Her father . . . Cielo Hermoso.* She sighed, searching for a strength she wasn't sure she possessed.

Cleve was looking at her, offering her his arm. "What do you say?" he asked.

Reluctantly at first, but with gathering spirit, Charlotte let herself be led into the dance. Once the music surrounded her, once she saw the haughty, triumphant look on Rose's face, her feet began to move with a life of their own. As if her body, too, had a memory of its own, she began to move in rhythm to the music.

As the dance ended, another partner came to take Cleve's place, then another and another. Sad as she was, Charlotte could not help smiling. They were her friends, showing their loyalty to her. They would not let Rose Fontaine humiliate her at her own party. Soon, while Charlotte still had young men begging for their first dance with her, Rose ran out of partners. Only her fiancé would dance with her, and though she tried to pretend she was happy about it, everyone could see that she wasn't.

For a few moments at a time, lost in the music and dancing, Charlotte would forget about Juan. Then his memory would come flooding back to her, and her heart would feel as if a hundred cactus needles were jabbing into it. Why couldn't she forget him? Why couldn't she concentrate on the wonderful, flattering things Jim Richter was whispering into her ear?

Then, suddenly, over the top of Jim's shoulder, she saw something that almost made her stumble. *Juan!* It was his form, his tall silhouette, gliding in the shadows. But no, she told herself, no, it couldn't be. Juan was gone, a hundred miles away. Juan would never come into her life again.

But there he was. There was no mistake now. It was Juan, striding toward her through the dancers. Without a word he took her away from Jim Richter. Without a word Jim Richter faded into the background as if he had never existed.

It took Charlotte a moment to catch her breath, a moment to get over the dizzying, delicious feeling of being held in Juan's arms. "What . . . what are you doing here? Your father said—I thought—"

"Ssh, *querida*," he whispered in her ear, his warm breath sending a shiver through her body. "Ssh."

So Charlotte said nothing for the remainder of the dance. Everyone watching her—Teyah and Maggie and her father, Jim Richter and Cleve and Rose Fontaine herself—saw the transformation that occurred. As she danced with Juan, Charlotte began to glow. By the time the dance ended, Charlotte alone, Charlotte without a single ruby or pearl or diamond, was more radiant than Rose Fontaine in all her jewels.

"Darn!" Rose whispered, but no one was paying any attention to her.

On the far side of the dance floor Charlotte was looking into Juan's eyes. "I feel as if everyone's watching us," she said "Can we go somewhere where we'll be alone?"

A few minutes later they were standing far from the party, alone in a moon-swept pasture. Everything was so perfect, so absolutely perfect, she was almost afraid to speak. But she had to, and looking up, she asked, "What are you doing here, Juan? Your father said you left last night."

"I did," Juan said. "I got almost to the new land, to the place I bought to build our ranch on. Then I realized there will be no ranch without you, Charlotte. No house, no barns, not without you. I love you, *querida*. I had to come back. Maybe you cannot part with Cielo Hermoso, but I cannot part with you. That is how it is."

Charlotte's heart began to beat rapidly. She could hardly believe her ears. "Juan, are you saying—"

"That we will live on Cielo Hermoso, if that is what you wish."

Charlotte flung her arms around him and hugged him to her, hugged him so tightly she could feel his heart beating against hers. "Oh,

Juan, I love you so much. I've never loved anyone else, never, and I never will."

He kissed her, his arms scooping her up and lifting her against him so that her feet, in their little satin slippers, left the earth. "Does that mean that you will marry me, *querida*?"

"Yes, oh, yes, Juan, I'll marry you and we'll live—"

She stopped abruptly. She'd been about to say, "We'll live at Cielo Hermoso." But suddenly she couldn't say it. Why hadn't she realized it before? Juan, the Juan she knew and loved, would never be happy at Cielo Hermoso. Her father had been right. A man like Juan needed to stand on his own feet. If she tried to change him, he would never be happy. And suddenly his happiness mattered more to her than anything. It mattered even more than Cielo Hermoso.

"What is it, Charlotte?" Juan asked.

"I just realized something," she said with a little shake of her head.

"What?"

"I just realized what love is. Oh, Juan, I don't want to live at Cielo Hermoso. I want to live on the new land, with you. I want you to build me the biggest, the most beautiful ranch in Texas."

For a moment he simply looked at her. Then a smile broke across his face, and he pulled her to him. "You are loco," he whispered in her ear as he kissed her cheek. His lips wandered over her cheek to her nose, to her closed eyelids, to the little wisps of hair at her forehead. "You are crazy and unpredictable, and I will never, never understand you; but I will marry you anyway, Charlotte, and I will build you the most magnificent ranch in all of Texas. You will never be sorry."

Hidden Longings 151

"No," she murmured, opening her eyes just long enough to see his dark eyes above her, "I will never be sorry. There's just one thing, Juan."

"And what is that?"

"Our horse business. I want to go on with it. We can build new stables. Why not, as long as we have to build everything else? I already own Lisette and her mother, and father will give us horses for our wedding present if we ask, I know he will, and—"

"And what about the stables we built together?" Juan asked, holding her close. "I suppose you will want to pull them apart board by board and move them to our new ranch."

Charlotte shook her head. "No. I spoke to Cleve. He knows a lot about horses, too, you know, and he wants to start a business of his own. He offered to buy Lisette from me, but I refused, of course. Anyway, our stables will be in good hands. Cleve and Teyah will make good use of them. Father has agreed to the arrangement. He knows that I'll only be happy if I'm with you—I think he knew it before I did."

Juan grinned. He was sure his father felt the same way George Harmon did.

"And as long as we're going to have more land," Charlotte continued, "why not build stables that are even bigger than these?"

Juan chuckled softly, his breath tickling her ear. "Could it be, *querida*, that you just want to outdo Cielo Hermoso?"

"Of course not," Charlotte replied swiftly. "It's just the horses I'm thinking of."

Juan sighed. "As I said, you are stubborn and unpredictable. But if you want to raise horses on our ranch, we will raise horses on our ranch. Horses and cattle."

Charlotte nodded. Soon they would go back to the party; they would tell her father that they were going to get married and move off to the new country. But for right now all that existed were Juan and the moonlight and the grass that swayed and whispered around them like a restless ocean. Those things and the love they had for each other, a love that, for the moment, seemed larger and more powerful than anything else in the world.

STARFIRE

Out of the Romantic Past Comes

TEXAS PROMISES

Set against the wild backdrop of Texas in the 1860s, here are two books, full of excitement and romance, about three beautiful young women dealing with the harsh realities of frontier life and reveling in the promise of love.

Strongwilled Maggie McNeill is determined to make a success of the family ranch and win the heart of adventurous Buck Crawford. A danger-filled 700-mile cattle drive becomes the scene of Maggie's dramatic efforts.

☐ **DREAMS AT DAWN:** TEXAS PROMISES: **BOOK I**

Headstrong Charlotte Harmon, pampered and elegant, has to work hard for the first time in her life when disaster strikes the Harmon stables. And making an impression on the elusive Juan Ortiz isn't easy either. But Charlotte is used to winning—*nothing* is going to stand in her way.   26289/$2.50

☐ **UNTAMED HEART:** TEXAS PROMISES: **BOOK II**

Restless, impulsive Teyah, half-Apache, half-white, strikes out on her own searching desperately for a place where she can belong. Cleve Harmon knows Teyah's place is in his heart, but it's going to take a lot to convince Teyah of that.   26474/$2.50